Dead Like Stars

Dead Like Stars

BOOK ONE OF THE BLOODLIFE SERIES

Anastasia Poirier

liquididea press

PORTLAND, OREGON

Dead Like Stars
Copyright © 2017 Anastasia Poirier

Edited by Dario Ciriello
Cover by Derek Murphy

For updates, mailing list, and future releases, please visit AnastasiaPoirier.com.

ISBN: 978-1-942097-05-1

Keywords: Dark Fantasy, Female Protagonist, Feelings & Emotions, Physical & Emotional Abuse, Dark Comedy, Vampire, Occult Fiction, Myths and Legends.

For everyone who encouraged me to keep writing, and to you, reader. Thank you.

Chapter 1

Cleaning coffee rings from tables is a perfect metaphor for my life; gone in an instant with hardly a struggle. Every second I spend here, making lattes for people who've never worked a service job in their life, is a waste. They never consider that the chick frothing their milk is an actual person with dreams and aspirations . . . or I would have these things, if I wasn't stuck here.

My coworker Lisa doesn't like to talk about dreams or life or anything other than men she finds attractive, but right now, she's silent, probably texting some guy or three instead of putting the mugs away and cleaning the espresso machine so we can leave. The reality is worse: she's reading one of those celebrity gossip magazines. I know because of the look on her face—lips parted, eyes round and staring. It's the same look rubberneckers get when driving past a car accident. They want to see blood.

I really should stop her; once she starts, it'll take weeks to get her back to normal. She'll be telling me about the latest couples in Hollywood, identifying them with cutesy name mash-ups. I'd rather hear her gag-worthy sexual adventures, at least they're imaginative.

It's this place. We both need to get out. No time like the present. My stomach tingles like I'm about to leap from a cliff, and I just know I'm about to do something reckless, but it's exciting too. "I quit."

"Uh huh." Lisa doesn't look up. "Most of this stuff's crap, but I can almost believe this. Michael Jackson really did look like an alien." The paper rustles as she turns the page.

I toss my towel on the table. Muffled voices from the television mounted behind the counter clutter the silence. "I'm going to give birth to kittens and move to Mars."

"Oh my god! This is unbelievable. Duh! Of course I want to see the autopsy photos." Her outburst makes me jump, but she's not listening. She turns another page and snorts laughter. "Oh, man. You gotta look at this—"

I march across the cafe and tear the magazine from her hands. Michael Jackson gazes up from the cover with giant purple alien eyes. "You know these things cause brain damage, right?"

She grins, finally looking at me, a sheet of wavy blonde hair hiding half of her pixie face. "Yeah, yeah, but only after prolonged exposure. Luckily, I have you to pull me back from the brink."

"You didn't hear a word I said, did you?"

Her face scrunches. "Something about kittens? My brain cells were busy with all the dying."

"I'm quitting."

"What?" She straightens, and her face goes serious. "Why? Because of Rick? Come on, Sasha. So he grabbed your ass a few times. Big deal."

"Big deal?" I shudder. Just thinking about him makes my skin crawl. I should have left months ago, but change sucks, and it's not like there's anything but more of the same on the horizon.

"It's not that bad." Lisa flings her hair over her shoulder. "It's like a compliment, especially for you. He usually doesn't go for the Wednesday Addams type."

"Thanks, I just threw up in my mouth." Of course she would put it that way, like sexual objectification is a privilege.

Lisa cranks the espresso machine's steam wand full blast and polishes it vigorously—and sensuously, the way she always does when the conversation turns to Rick. I'm glad her face is obscured behind the billowing steam; I'm sure she's making obscene faces. If I show even a hint of disgust she'll start in with the moaning.

I cross to the door, switch off the open sign, and lock the door. No one will notice if we close fifteen minutes early. Business is slow in February anyway. No one wants to brave the torrential storms, especially when it's this dark by four forty-five.

Mugs clatter as Lisa stacks them on top of the espresso machine. She has moved on, then; no more porno polishing for now, but she's giving me the silent treatment. She'll get over it. I brush past her into the cramped office, scrawl, *Rick, I quit. — Sasha Rigel,* on a sticky note, and slap it in the center of the computer screen where he'll find it in the morning.

It feels like victory.

As I exit the office, Lisa looks up from the TV. Her face is serious again, strained. She's turned up the volume and raises her voice to be heard. "Have you seen the news?" Her mouth bows in a frown.

"Life's depressing enough without being barraged with the horrors of humanity at the top of every hour." Only masochists watch the news.

Lisa rolls her eyes and points at the TV. A woman with sleek dark hair and a smart-looking suit fills the screen. Below her, white letters against a red background read: 'Update: Total missing jumps to seventy-five.'

"Missing—"

"Shh!" Lisa flaps her hand at me and increases the volume. I resist the urge to cover my ears, and find myself leaning closer to the screen despite the noise.

The newswoman's stuffy voice fills the empty coffee shop. "—authorities are not giving us much. At present, there's no connection between the missing, but they've all vanished from the metro area. The Portland police are asking anyone with information to come forward—"

Lisa looks back at me, her eyes wide. "Did you see that? Seventy-five. Just last week it was thirty."

I shrug, but inside my guts are twisting. It's nothing, people go missing all the time, and most of them are assholes anyway, right?

"Seriously? You're not worried?"

If I were honest, I'd tell her my problem is I worry too much, but I'm not honest. I drop the volume to a whisper. "It's just drugs. They're blowing it way out of proportion to boost ratings."

"This has nothing to do with drugs or ratings. It's real people." Lisa fixes me with a holier-than-thou stare—as if she hadn't just been reading brain-melting tabloids.

"Real people? As opposed to what, fake ones? Are you suggesting victims of the drug trade aren't real?" I bite my cheek to keep from laughing.

Her eyes narrow. "You know what I mean. Guys, chicks, kids—freaking librarians!"

"What is it this time, then? A super prolific serial killer—do they have a Guinness record for that yet? Maybe it's equal opportunity sex traffickers. Finally, right?" My laughter shrivels up. She's giving me that look. I've gone too far.

Her arms fold over her thin chest and her head does that thing she does when she's angry—a tilt to the left, and all I see is the cocker spaniel my parents had—and I pinch myself hard to keep a smile off my face.

"Everything's a morbid joke with you! This is serious." Her voice wavers like she might cry, and I look down. An ant hauls a crumb of muffin across the tile. I want to step on him, crush him like my feelings.

"I know . . . I'm sorry." And I am sorry. Sorry that suffering triggers my snark. As if sarcasm can make the world less horrifying.

She takes a deep breath and lets it out in a harsh sigh. "No. It's fine. I wish I could be more like you. You're not scared of anything. It's just got me all worked up. One guy was last seen just up the street from here."

My ego likes that she thinks I'm fearless, but it only shows how little she really knows me. But that's not her fault. No one knows me. "Great. Now I'm paranoid. See, this is why I don't follow the news." I grab my coat from the cabinet below the TV. "I have to walk home in fear now, thanks to you."

"You'll be fine," she says with a wicked grin. "They only take people, not heartless androids." She laughs and switches off the TV. She has forgiven me, again. "You coming to Vox tonight?"

It would be good to get out—far better than moping around my apartment worrying about job interviews and serial killers. "Yeah. Sure," I say as I walk to the door.

"It'll be fun! You can find a pretty goth boy and have job breakup sex! Jeremy's single . . ." She bites her lip and shrugs. "Well, he's single-ish. I'd do him."

I'd be surprised if she hasn't already. Jeremy has been through more than half the scene. If he were in the dictionary his definition would say, see *cesspool*. What was the saying? When you sleep with someone, you sleep with everyone they've been with. I suppress a shiver and glance at Lisa over my shoulder, one eyebrow raised.

She laughs and throws up her hands. "Yeah, I know. You're antisexual and you hate fun—or whatever. See you tonight."

❀ ❀ ❀

My apartment is a small basement studio, but it's cozy, or at least that's what the ad said. As if anything situated directly behind an abortion clinic can be considered cozy. Convenient maybe, if you have a need for that sort of thing, but the protesters squash any possibility of comfort.

It isn't all bad though. There's one window—complete with heavy iron bars—which provides a flattering shin-level view of passersby. Those bars decrease the odds of some wacko breaking in while I sleep but increase my odds of burning to death in a fire. I consider that a win. This city is full of wackos, a few of them are my exes. That's precisely why I've given up dating. Who has time anyway? I have too many books to read, too much tea to drink and my Netflix queue is out of control.

I turn on the shower, imagining the hot pink sticky note clinging to Rick's computer screen. It's surreal, like a dream. I've never straight up quit before. I've always had a backup plan.

At first it was liberating, but now panic is creeping in, gnawing like a starving rat. I'll have to start the job search again and face all those mind-numbing interview questions. My personal favorite: *Tell me about a time when you gave exceptional customer service.* I can never think of an appropriate response. There's a million sarcastic ones: I remade a woman's latte three times because the temperature wasn't *just* right, and I refrained from punching the insufferable bitch. How's that for customer service?

I groan and let the hot water run over my face. I'd almost rather die. Perhaps it isn't too late to un-quit? My old lockpicks are around here somewhere. I could break in, throw my note away . . .

And continue getting groped and eye-raped every day? No, thanks. I've made my decision. Tomorrow it's back into the wonderful world of unemployment, but tonight I'll be enduring Lisa's constant attempts to hook me up with every available, or semi-available guy. I don't know which I'm looking forward to less.

❀ ❀ ❀

My closet is a sea of black. A lone red shirt lurks at the back, bright, an explosion in the void of space. A monochromatic wardrobe might be boring to some, but it sure takes the guesswork out of matching—unless you're picky about matching blacks. I'm not.

I take a sip of tea from my cup on the dresser. I just made it, but it's cold already; story of my life. Then I realize that was yesterday's tea . . . or is it from last week? Gross. I gather three mugs, none of them from today—my current tea has apparently traveled to another dimension—and deposit them in the kitchen sink.

Returning to my closet, a faded Better Beings t-shirt catches my eye, but I know I should try harder. I wear jeans and a band shirt every day. I'll put in some effort, but I draw the line at fancy panties—I don't care *that* much.

I wrestle a skirt from the bottom dresser drawer. I haven't worn a skirt in years—Lisa will shit herself. But, holding it to my waist, I see it's far too short. Did I ever really wear this? I toss it back in the drawer and choose a plain black corset: appropriately revealing while still covering everything, or, mostly everything. It's the most effort I've put into my appearance in months; I'll never hear the end of it.

Several minutes later, my arms are numb, but my tits look great. I haven't decided if that's a good thing. Solitary corset donning should qualify as an Olympic sport. It requires coordination to pull all those strings behind your back while holding your breath. I make a mental note to email someone about it and return to the bathroom for some primping. I dry my hair, smudge on some eyeliner, and, for good measure, add some lipstick too. Black—like my soul. Ha!

Chapter 2

A black cargo van rolls to a stop outside a steel and brick warehouse, and a motion-activated floodlight blinks on. The harsh light barely penetrates the van's darkly tinted windows, exposing only shadows of the two inside. The passenger door opens and a woman steps out. She jerks a heavy robe over her high-collared, white uniform and tucks her matted blonde hair into the hood as she makes her way to the front of the van. She pauses before the warehouse's steel double doors, and a look of what might be annoyance flashes across her face, her violet eyes narrowing for an instant before she turns to the sound of the driver's door closing.

The driver is masculine with a smooth, bare head, but he looks like something pretending to be a man—it's his eyes, dark, possibly black like those of a demon in a horror movie. Like his partner, his skin is so pale, it's nearly indistinguishable from the luminescent whiteness of his uniform over which he straightens his own grey robe, then flips the hood up before stopping at the woman's side. He is taller by a foot and it takes her a moment to find his face, just a fraction of a second, as if she expects someone closer to her own height. Their eyes meet and the light finds its way beneath his hood. His eyes aren't black but violet, the same color as the woman's, yet different: apart from the color, her eyes pass for human, but his are solid, insectile, pupilless. He glances down at her, the skin between his non-existent eyebrows pinches together, and they speak in an unknown, harsh language—their voices soft and feminine, eerily similar—then he slips through the double doors into the warehouse while she circles to the rear of the van and opens the doors.

The hold of the van is bare metal; the floor has dark patches of rust or maybe dried blood. At one time there may have been carpet and seats but they're missing now. A heavy wire mesh separates the back from the cab.

Hardly two minutes pass before the warehouse doors swing open. The tall man in grey steps out, and a procession of people follow, single file, their faces blank, necks and shirts smeared with blood. They cross the few feet of asphalt to the rear of the van, where the robed woman shoves them into the van.

A brunette woman of perhaps thirty stumbles; the robed figure catches her by the hair and yanks her upright with incredible force, then pushes her into the hold. The brunette's face remains blank—even as she scuffs her knees on the bare metal—and the others already in the van take no notice; no one offers help, and she doesn't wait; she picks herself up and shuffles to the back, pressing in against the others to make room.

The robed woman hesitates, her fist bunched in a man's sweatshirt, squints at a streak of blood on the back of her hand. She pushes the man in, casually wiping her hand clean on the front of the next person's shirt, a slight grimace twisting her pale lips.

The van fills rapidly, even though the vacant people pack in close, and still more people file out of the warehouse. The robed figures don't seem concerned. Their calm demeanor suggests they've done this before, many times.

❖ ❖ ❖

Heavy bass seeps from Vox across the street. Lisa's out front, flirting with a guy with streaks of neon green makeup on half his face like war paint. She leans on him, her arms hooked around his neck. The hem of her skimpy black skirt has crept up, and I'm pretty sure she's not wearing underwear. She's putting on a show for all of Eleventh Street. I doubt she cares.

I step from the curb, and a black van appears out of nowhere. It brakes and swerves, tires screeching, barely missing me. I leap back, my heart hammering.

"Watch where you're going, fuckface!" Never mind that I should heed my own advice. Had I even looked before hopping off the curb like a lemming? But that's reason, and it's too late for reason. I snatch a rock from the gutter and hurl it after the van. The stone chinks off the tinted rear window. It's too small to do any damage, but the brake lights glare and the van jerks to a stop. Reverse lights flash.

Oh, this'll be good. A nagging voice whispers I should run—people carry guns—but I'm full of adrenaline and itching for a fight. I compose an acid response to fling in the driver's face; something about how the world would be better if their mother had access to more effective methods of birth control. But as the blacked-out passenger side window descends, words—and everything else for that matter—melt.

Run! Scream for help. Do something, anything.

I can only stare at the two . . . beings . . . in the cab. They both wear dark grey robes, high white collars peek out from beneath. The passenger is androgynous with matted white hair like dreadlocks gone wrong, but the driver is clearly not human.

11

Its eyes slide over me, and even in the gloomy interior, I'm struck by its buggy violet eyes: shockingly similar to the photoshopped image of alien Michael Jackson from the cover of Lisa's magazine. The driver's gaze continues over its shoulder, coming to rest on a steel mesh barrier separating the cab from the back of the van. From behind the screen, I see movement. People. Silent, blank-faced people are stuffed in the back.

Muscle control and my sense of self-preservation return, but not fast enough. The passenger leans toward me. I'm relieved that she doesn't have the same bug-eyes as the driver, then I notice that though her eyes appear normal, this close it's clear that her irises are the same intense shade as the driver's. Before I can take more than a step back, the passenger's arm whips out, catching my coat, and I'm reeled in so quickly that I slam against the door. The air rushes from my lungs and my hip throbs. I'll have a massive bruise by morning—assuming I live that long.

I draw a breath to scream, and she, *is it a she?* tilts her head and pinches the air with her free hand. When I do scream, no sound comes out. It's as if my voice is pinched between her bony fingers.

Her mouth quirks in an almost-smile, and she makes a shushing sound. "Be calm. You will wait. Stay." Her voice is strange, almost feminine, but also distorted and slightly mechanical.

I freeze against the door. I have a feeling like I've forgotten something. Something I needed to do—*Wait.* I was going somewhere—*Stay.*

The two beings speak to each other in a strange language. The driver glances once more over its shoulder at the people crammed in the back and subtly shakes his head. I should be scared, but—*Calm.*

12

The woman—creature?—holding me, speaks again. "Arm."

My mind empties, and my left arm extends into the cab. Cold, clammy fingers force my sleeve back, and a cold metallic disk presses against my upturned forearm. The disk blinks once, a blinding red flash in the dark of the cab, then pain, searing agony. I can't pull away. I can't scream. My skin reddens and blisters as the disk bores in. Then it's gone, buried. The blisters lessen and disappear, and the redness fades.

"Close your eyes," my captor whispers.

I obey. My arm is released and I hug it to my chest.

"You will forget this."

A gust of wind from a passing van blows my hair back from my face, and I gasp. I nearly stepped off the curb into its path. I'd been absorbed in thought, just placing one foot in front of the other: a great way to get myself creamed. What had I been thinking? I scratch absently at my left arm, check for cars, and continue across the street.

"Sasha!"

Lisa is jumping up and down across the street, waving at me, her violet lipstick bright against her fair skin. The color makes me shiver. No, that's stupid. It's just the cold. I hug my coat closer and trot to her side, shoving aside my latest mental episode. *Hi, I'm Sasha. Violet makes me nervous-sweat.*

"Who was that in the van?" Lisa asks, shimmying her eyebrows.

"What van?" I turn back to the street. There's the usual Friday night traffic, but not a van in sight.

"It was a man, wasn't it?" She pokes a finger into my ribs. "Come on, you can tell me."

"What are you on?" What man is she talking about? I bat her hand away and squint into her eyes. Are her pupils dilated? Maybe just a bit.

She laughs and pushes me away. "Jesus, Sash. If you don't want to tell, that's fine, whatever."

"There's nothing to tell. If there was a guy, you'd be the first to know." She would likely know before I did.

"Okay," she says, placated for the moment. "I'm glad you came. I was sure you'd flake like last week and the week before."

She says it like she cares, but I know she doesn't. She's only concerned about which guys will show up. I don't take it personally. Tonight, I just want to dance and have all my thoughts obliterated by loud music.

She tugs at my coat. "Dang! Look at that. Showing some cleavage tonight, huh?"

"So what?" I smack her hands away and pull my coat closed. I knew she would have to say something.

She gives me a devilish grin. "You're *so* trying to get a guy."

She has a one-track mind tonight. She and Dave must be on the outs again. "A girl can't show a little cleavage without someone thinking she's on the prowl? If anything, this is a dude deterrent. Do you know how long it takes to get this thing off?"

"Suuure." She laughs and pats my arm.

I want to scream at her, *Would I be wearing these holey full-butt panties if I were trying to pick someone up?* but there are too many people around for that sort of confession. I push her hands away. "Whatever. Let's go in. It's freezing out here."

We half jog to the entrance and show our IDs to the stern-faced man at the door. He gives us a bored look and waves us in. The muffled music grows louder until we're enveloped in sound. Bass pounds in my chest like an artificial heart, making it hard to breathe. Colored spotlights flit across the room, punching holes in the darkness. People encased in vinyl, corsets, and black leather huddle on couches, their painted faces veiled in the shifting light. On the dance floor, bodies thrash like swarms of angry bees.

I lead the way, weaving through the crowd. It's like that old game Frogger, only instead of dodging cars, I dodge flailing people, and the result of a collision is a fate worse than death: a slimy sheen of stranger sweat. I cringe, hugging my hands to my chest, and resist the urge to sprint for the safety of the vacant nook directly in front of the massive speakers.

At last, we make it. I ball up my coat and wedge it between the speaker and the wall.

"There are a lot of cute guys here tonight," Lisa shouts over the music.

I glance around and shrug. It's the same people every week. At least none of my exes are here. Then again, the night is young—there's plenty of time for awkward encounters.

"You're impossible! Did you see the new bartender?"

I look past the crowd at the small bar on the far side of the room. A thick-chested man with a dark goatee and a smooth, bald head hustles behind the counter. I wrinkle my nose. "He's all yours."

She strips off her coat and bunches it up on top of mine. "I need a drink." She waggles her eyebrows and strides off toward the bar.

I close my eyes and try to shut everyone out. I can only dance if I pretend I'm alone. It's hard to start. My knees shake and my feet are lead. It's this struggle that often keeps me home, but the relief that comes with pushing past my fear and expressing myself, even just this little bit, is worth it. I like to think of it as therapy, a safe outlet—my only outlet. I can't talk to anyone. Lisa wouldn't care, and boyfriends . . . no. Trusting their fumbling hands with my body is risky enough. Feelings aren't something to be discussed with men, no matter how much they insist they love me. Nothing can be solved with words or the airing of irrational feelings anyway. I need something physical that won't land me in the hospital. So I dance.

I'm pulled from my thoughts when a sweaty guy brushes against me. I recoil, he grins and attempts a wink. I hope his face freezes like that. A can of cheap beer sloshes in his fist as he shouts something to me over the music. He dances closer, and I shoot him a dirty look that I hope conveys that I wish him a slow and violent death. His sloppy grin falters, but he rebounds quickly, shifting his sights to the next female.

Where is Lisa? She's supposed to deflect these guys for me. I scan the dance floor, but there's no sign of her. From the corner of my eye, I see beer-slosher has found a willing dance partner. They writhe together in a sickening display of drunken sexual tension. People are so weird.

I look past them at the crowd gathered around the bar. Still no Lisa, instead I see three chads loitering around the far corner, chugging cheap beer and drunkenly shouting come-ons at every female-presenting person who walks by. I can hear them over the music. They really should be kicked out—but that would imply someone gives a shit.

The enormous crew cut blonde in the orange Polo must be the ringleader. He dishes the majority of the catcalls while the other two laugh and clap him on the shoulder like he's won a prize. Even from across the room, something in that one's eyes makes my skin crawl.

My gaze shifts to a man at the opposite end of the bar. He's pale—big surprise with this crowd—long dark hair falls just past his narrow shoulders. It's a nice change from the shorter, swoop-with-shaved-sides look most goth men sport these days, it's more of a classic look. He watches the group of catcalling chads with open contempt.

Laughter erupts from the group, no doubt at some woman's expense. I almost turn back to glare at them, but I can't stop staring at this new guy. My head swims, and I realize I'm holding my breath. I want to look away, I need to; if I don't he'll notice, then he'll come talk to me, and I can't. The last thing I need is another ex—more drama. But it's too late. His eyes meet mine, and his lips twitch. It might have been a smile, but it was so brief, and now his face is serious, his eyes intense, boring into mine even across the distance. I swallow hard and turn around, my cheeks burning.

I shut my eyes and try to lose myself in the music, but I can only see him. I imagine that twitch of a smile. Had it been a smile? Perhaps it was a grimace? His lips looked soft.

My preoccupation with him is ridiculous. He nags at my thoughts, burrowing deeper. Seeping, like poison, because he could only be poison. They say you always date your father. It's no wonder my love life is so fucked up.

My eyes creep back to his spot near the bar; I'm helpless to stop them. He's gone. I don't know if I want to sigh with relief or cry in despair, and this realization brings another wave of self-loathing. How pathetic: a victim of my own stupid hormones. I'm no better than Lisa. This is all her fault, with her talk of pretty goth boys.

A hand closes on my shoulder, and I jump.

Lisa tosses her head back, laughing. "Jeez, Sash. It's just me. Did I miss something?"

"Huh?"

"You look like a lemur scouting for danger."

My face grows hot. Was I that obvious? "I was just looking for you." Just a small lie. I adjust my corset and resist the urge to scan the crowd over her shoulder. "How'd it go with Anton LaVey?" I tip my head to the bar.

17

"The Satanic Bible guy?" She squints at the bartender and laughs. "He does kinda look like him. It's the goatee, I think. So hot, and look at the size of those hands! I bet just one could wrap all the way around my—"

I know where this is going, straight into I-don't-want-to-know territory. "Anyway . . ."

She makes her *I'm sorry you're such a prude* face, and flips her hair to one side. "Yeah, anyway. He hardly said two words to me, the jerk." She brings her glass to her lips, and her tiny, perfect teeth clamp on the straw. "He's so gay."

"He'd have to be to resist your charms," I say, shaking my head.

She smirks around her straw, and her eyes flit over my shoulder. "Oh, look! Dave's here!"

"I thought you guys broke up again."

"Yeah, we're just friends now, you know." She waggles her eyebrows. I hate it when she does that. "Friends with benefits."

"Barf."

"Hey, don't knock it." She drains her drink in one epic slurp.

"So you're over his hillbilly sideburns?"

"It's rockabilly." Her face contorts and she gags. "They're still repulsive, but hey, that's why blindfolds were invented." She shrugs one shoulder, thumps her empty glass down on a speaker, and saunters off, doing her *come fuck me* hip wiggle.

I roll my eyes at her back and plop down on a couch at the edge of the dance floor. Lisa has it easy: her confidence, her take-nothing-seriously attitude. Sometimes I wonder if being more like her would solve all my problems. Sometimes.

I catch myself staring at the dark nook by the bar. I wasn't looking for him. No way. He's repulsive, definitely a creeper. It's just the club lighting. It can make just about anyone attractive at first glance, not to mention all this fog. Besides, I swore I'd never date a pretty guy again, not after last time. This guy is leagues beyond my ex, but that only exponentially increases his crazy factor. Is it even possible to be crazier than my ex? He'd have to be a serial killer or a cannibal. Yes: A serial-killing cannibal.

It's a valiant effort, but I still want him. Even if it's only good for a while. Hell, he's so incredibly gorgeous, even if it's the worst relationship ever—and it would be. It would be worth it. Maybe . . . probably.

Screw it. I've already done one crazy thing today. It's not like talking to him can be any worse than a job interview. It's like practice, really. Fine, if I see him again, I'll talk to him, and if he isn't too weird, then maybe . . . I bite my lip to keep from smiling, and suddenly I'm regretting the decision to wear these holey granny panties. Who am I?

The couch shifts, pulling me out of my thoughts, and I look over to see the chad in the orange shirt climbing over the back. He settles in beside me like he owns the place.

"What's up, Morticia? I bet you'd be hot without all that." He waves an arm in the general direction of my everything.

I glare, resisting the urge to shrink away from him. "Fuck off."

"What's that? You wanna suck my dick?" He grins.

His eyes are voids, and I try to imagine what's really going on behind them. What makes a person behave this way? Insecurity?

He carries on as if I'm not giving him the world's most searing death stare.

"Right here? Shit, girl. Say no more." His hands move to his belt and he throws a wink over my shoulder to where I'm sure his friends wait, watching the master at work.

I jump up from the couch, but he grabs my wrist. My stomach knots the instant his fingers close on my skin, and my pulse rises, pounding in my ears—drowning out the music. My vision blurs. I draw back to kick him but he yanks me off balance, and I stumble back to the couch.

His grip tightens, and the bones in my wrist grind together. A shrill whine escapes my lips; his dead eyes brighten and his grin widens. "Chill out. I was just messin'." His tone is casual, playful. It's meant to be disarming, but that look in his eyes is all too familiar.

"Let go of me." I mean it to come out strong, intimidating, but my voice betrays me. I can't breathe. My eyes squeeze shut. If I could just concentrate hard enough I could disappear, but I'm not a kid anymore, and I know that never works. It never has.

Crew Cut releases my wrist with a strangled yelp, and my eyes fly open. For a moment the world makes no sense. Crew Cut is hovering in front of me, his feet kicking uselessly from several inches off the ground. Then I see *him*—the long-haired guy from the bar—and though the two are nearly the same height, somehow this slim, elvish-looking man has this crew cut hulk suspended by the throat with one hand. His face is calm, as if holding Crew Cut is no effort at all, but his eyes . . . I've never seen such intensity, such pure hatred. His lips move, and the hulk in his grasp stops kicking.

After a long second, he sets Crew Cut down, and the chad scuttles away to join his friends. Even over Combichrist's harsh screams blaring from the speakers, I can hear the others howling with laughter at Crew Cut's expense, but it's nervous laughter. They saw the same thing I did and they want no part of it.

Slowly I become aware that he's still here. I see him from the corner of my eye, glaring at Crew Cut and his friends who cast furtive glances back at him, sizing him up. He's tall, bony, almost feminine, and I can almost hear their thoughts as they struggle to make sense of what just happened. Maybe they wonder if they could take him, perhaps together? In the end, they seem to have doubts, and they make their way toward the exit, no doubt off to harass someone else.

The new man still hasn't moved. Suddenly I'm angry, maybe because part of me thinks he's waiting for me to thank him, like he's a hero or something. Like I couldn't defend myself; I would have been fine. But really I'm mad because I'm still too scared to talk to him, afraid I'll say something stupid. It's easier to dismiss him, hate him even. How dare he assume I need help? I shake my head. I am completely irrational.

I want to hide, but it's too late—he's caught me looking again. This time he does smile, and somehow he seeps in past my defenses. Panic sweeps through me—fight or flight, and I'm all about flight—but my legs refuse to move. My heart crashes against my ribs as if it hopes to break free and fling itself flopping and naked at his feet. All over a smile, a pretty face. My hands are freezing and sweating all at once. What's wrong with me?

"It seems this seat is no longer taken. May I join you if I promise to behave?" His voice is rich with just a hint of an accent. Of course he's English.

I only nod; not trusting my treacherous voice.

He sits beside me, graceful as a cat, and offers his hand, the same one that seconds ago was clamped around a man's throat. "I'm Ambrose."

Ambrose? Great, he's one of *those*. This isn't an Anne Rice novel. I resist the urge to look around for a camera crew. This has to be a prank. Did Lisa set this up?

He's looking at me, one eyebrow raised, and I remember my manners, which have strangely decided to make an appearance for him. Not just because he's beautiful, I'm not *that* shallow, but there's something unassuming about him, alluring.

"Sasha." I take his hand and try to ignore how right his palm feels pressed against mine. I'm insane.

He turns my hand in his, hesitantly brushing his thumb across my knuckles, and I just know he's going to kiss it. Sure enough, he raises my hand to his lips, and I do nothing to stop him. What's worse, I don't want him to stop. My heart lurches as his lips graze my skin—they *are* soft.

My face is hot. I hope he can't tell in the dark, and I laugh to cover my embarrassment. Am I embarrassed because I like it or because it's just so goddamned awkward? Both? A voice in the back of my mind screams for me to get up, walk away. But I don't—can't—and my eyes flick up to his, so dark in the colored lights that they're nearly black. The tension eases from my shoulders and a contented sigh slips from my mouth. It's like the time the dentist gave me laughing gas when I was eight. Calm.

"Thanks for . . . you know." I tip my head toward the door. "You didn't have to."

"You're welcome." He drops his eyes to my hand, still held in his, and silence, amid all the noise of the club, stretches between us. I'm searching for something to say when at last, his head pops up. He's got that look in his eyes, the one that usually inspires my inner bitch, the one guys get before they utter something sappy, usually in hopes of getting into my pants.

"I don't mean to flatter, but you're one of the most beautiful women I've ever seen."

Men are all the same. I roll my eyes and shift, self-conscious. I want to pull my hand away. I want to punch him, and at the same time, I hate myself for hoping he's sincere. "You must not get out much."

He smiles guiltily. "You're right, I don't. It seems I have missed much."

A lock of dark hair falls across his face, and I want to brush it aside. I want to feel his lips again. My eyes drop to our hands. I'm losing this battle.

Lisa appears out of the fog, a question in her smile and surprise in her eyes. I yank my hand from his and spring from the couch, straightening my corset, smoothing my hair. I feel rumpled, like I've been doing more than talking. "Uh, hey, Lisa. This is Ambrose." My voice is thin, like I'm hiding something.

"Well, hello." She extends her hand to him, a predatory smile stretching her lips.

Ambrose stands. His arm brushes mine as he shakes her hand, and he gives her a polite smile. I wait for him to kiss her hand as well, snidely hoping he will. But he doesn't, and I silently rejoice. He's passed the douchebag test. For now.

He glances down at me; a smile flickers the corner of his mouth. Panic floods my chest. Why does he keep looking at me like I've said something amusing? Did I say something out loud? "What?"

"Hmm?" His slight smile retreats, and he gives me a confused look that seems contrived.

What am I thinking? It's not like he can read my mind. I'm totally insane: I quit my job, I've got half my tits hanging out, I'm talking to strange men. Yep, it's time to go home before I add anything else to this list.

Lisa tugs me aside, maybe sensing my urge to flee, and holds a finger up to Ambrose in the universally understood gesture for *Hold on one second*. Her rubbing alcohol breath puffs against my cheek as she shouts in my ear. "Are you going home with him?"

"What? Jesus, no!" I wish she would keep her voice down. I resist the urge to glance back at Ambrose. Can he hear her?

She pulls back, glances at Ambrose, then her impish grin is back. "Can I?"

If I could kill with my eyes. "Are you ser—"

"Just joking, god! Don't get your panties in a twist. He's too pretty anyway. Probably gay."

"Just because a guy doesn't throw himself at your feet—"

"Oh, hey, speaking of gay. You know Melanie, right?"

The sudden switch makes me blink, and I have to repeat her words in my head. "Melanie . . ."

I'm about to shake my head when Lisa blurts, "You know, giant boobs Melanie."

I nod hesitantly, this can't be good. "Your stripper friend?" I'm not sure I want to know where she's going with this. Sure, I vaguely know Melanie, but who the fuck cares?

"The preferred term is *entertainer*. Stripper is so demeaning."

I didn't think *demeaning* was even a concept in Lisa's depraved world. "Oh, and calling her *giant boobs Melanie* isn't?"

She sighs like I'm a lost cause. "Hey, I'm trying to help you here. She says she can get you a job."

I can see it now . . . Not. "I'm not dancing naked for money."

Lisa gives me her best *bitch, please* look. I'm not sure if I should be insulted. I could strip if I wanted to.

"No, not dancing, you're too pasty for that. They need a breakfast cook."

"Breakfast?"

"Eggs and legs!" She laughs at her own wit, and I nearly pull a muscle trying not to roll my eyes. "I told Mel you'll come by on Tuesday."

Oh, joy. Well, there's a bright side: I could get hit by a car and die between now and Tuesday. Here's to hoping.

"You can thank me later." She claps me on the shoulder and drags me back toward Ambrose, who, fortunately—unfortunately?—hasn't run off. "Anyway, you kids have fun. Me and Dave are cutting out early. His roomie's outta town." She leans over and shout-whispers in my ear, "Dave got a sex swing."

I gag. "You're oversharing again." I so hope Ambrose didn't hear that, but I know he did: he's barely holding back an amused smirk.

She rolls her eyes, nudges my shoulder, and whispers, more quietly this time, "Don't do anything I wouldn't do."

Right, that doesn't leave much. "Okay, bye." I push her toward Dave, who's standing a few paces away, stroking his revolting sideburns, looking eager to be off. Ready to break in the new swing, no doubt. I'll never get that visual out of my head.

"Bye, Ambrose. Nice meeting you." She turns to me "Call me tomorrow, Sash—not too early though. And remember, Tuesday!" She waves, hooks a finger in Dave's belt, and yanks him along behind her toward the exit.

I turn back to Ambrose, relieved she left before she could embarrass me further. "Sorry about her. She's boy crazy."

"You're not?" he asks with a sly smile.

I shrug. "I can appreciate a beautiful man, but they don't come around often. When they do, nature balances their good looks with insanity." The subtle, *scare them away* approach. Passive aggressive much?

"Is that so?"

He's not falling for it. "It's a pattern I've noticed. If I find someone attractive, they turn out to be insane, maladjusted to life's trauma. We all have issues, but some people just can't deal."

He is quiet for a moment, and I worry I've offended him—or I hope I've offended him, I'm not sure which—but then his voice lowers conspiratorially and he leans in, closing the distance between us. "Tell me, where am I on your crazy scale?"

My mind goes blank for a moment and his voice swims in my head. Then words are falling out of my mouth. "You're batshit. I shouldn't even be talking to you." I clap a hand over my mouth. My cheeks are burning again. "I'm sorry." Smooth. Is there anything else I'd like to blurt out? My heart races and my stomach is jumpy. He'll laugh now. I back away, preparing to flee as fast as my pride will allow. "Sorry . . . I have to go."

He touches my shoulder before I can turn away. His fingers are electric on my skin. "No. Stay. Dance with me. Please?"

I'm nodding before I even know I've changed my mind, and my heart slows. Why was I so spazzed out? It's only dancing. It's not like we're moving in together.

If dancing was hard earlier, it's impossible now. I'm hyperaware of every movement, his eyes on me. My legs shake and I'm sure that at any moment I'll trip over my boots and make a scene.

"Relax. Just dance." His voice is soft, and I shouldn't be able to hear him over the music, but his words are clear in my head. My legs stop wobbling, the tension leaves my shoulders, and suddenly the thought of him watching is kind of exciting.

❉ ❉ ❉

Two hours pass in a blur, and suddenly it's last call. Then the music fades from the speakers and the lights swell, exposing and blinding.

"Thanks for sharing your time with me." Ambrose's voice is too quiet. My ears are still throbbing from the loud music.

I open my mouth to respond, and I falter. He's even more beautiful in the light. Smooth, pale skin, a strong, yet feminine jaw and sharp cheekbones that give him a hungry, exotic look. But his eyes: they looked dark in the dim, colored lights, but they're violet. Just contacts, of course, and part of me wants to recoil in horror, but the color looks quite nice on him. What do I have against purple anyway? My breath catches and I know I've missed something because he's looking at me expectantly. My cheeks burn, but there's no hiding in this brightness. I drop my eyes to the floor and will my cheeks into compliance. "Sorry. What did you say?"

He waves a hand dismissively. "It's late. Let's get some fresh air."

The crisp air soothes my overheated skin. Soon I'm shivering, and Ambrose helps me into my coat.

"When can I see you again?" he asks.

I smile despite myself and shuffle my feet. I just know it's one of those idiotic smiles, a dog's smile. It feels too large, too eager. I bite the inside of my cheek to kill it. "I don't do this often . . ." I pat my pockets searching for my phone. "Or ever." Then I remember I left my phone charging on my nightstand. I tear a weathered band flyer off a nearby telephone pole and write my number on the back with my emergency stick of eyeliner. I thrust the paper into his hand and jerk away as if he might bite. "Call if you want." Yeah, way to play hard to get. Why don't I just tattoo *I want you* on my forehead?

That infuriating smile is on his face again. The corner of his mouth creases just slightly like there's some joke I'm missing.

"What? Why do you keep looking at me like that?"

"Looking at you like what?" His smile grows, lighting up his face, softening the sharp angles, stirring my traitorous heart. He has to know the effect of that smile.

I press on. "It's like you're laughing at me."

His face grows serious. "I apologize. I'm not laughing. I just feel lighter around you, but I'll work to contain myself."

I'm such a bitch. "No, you're fine. I'm just weird." A heavy sigh escapes my lips. "I better get home." Yes, get home before I do something stupid. I reach for his hand. "Nice meeting you."

He turns my hand in his and once again brings it to his lips, gazing down at me with his strange eyes. "Until next time."

❖ ❖ ❖

It's almost three a.m. and all the businesses are closed and dark. Traffic lights reflect off wet streets, tirelessly blinking through their colors. The passing cars on the distant highway whisper like breaking waves. I stare at the sidewalk, watching as each crack approaches and passes, my feet on autopilot homeward.

My thoughts turn to Ambrose. With each step, I'm more certain I imagined the whole encounter. He was too perfect. A little odd maybe—those violet contacts—but he didn't seem crazy. I should have asked for his number; at least then I'd have some proof of his existence.

Laughter and heavy footsteps interrupt the quiet, and I glance back. A group of men swagger up the sidewalk a few feet behind me. I catch a glimpse of an orange shirt and cropped blonde hair and do a double take.

"Hey, baby!" The big blonde yells.

Great, it's the same guy, though his speech is more slurred than it was a few hours ago. Does he recognize me? He makes wet, kissy noises, and the others laugh, high-fiving all around.

I quicken my pace, but their laughter pursues me, their footfalls coming more rapidly, echoing off the buildings. It's fine, don't overreact. They're just trying to scare me. What can they really do in the middle of the Pearl District? Half of these buildings are condos; someone will call the police if things get out of hand. Not to help me of course, but they can be counted on to protect their own quality of sleep.

"Yo! Girl! What's the rush?"

More laughter. Closer now.

I really should get a bike or something for these late night adventures. I bolt for Jamison Square, weaving through the skeleton trees along the strip of grass, but they're faster. Too late, I realize I'm being corralled.

I skid to a halt, slipping on the wet grass. The three of them fan out around me, their arms held low and wide like I'm a rabbit in the brush they hope to catch.

"What's the hurry? We just wanna—hey! It's the bitch from the freak club." Crew Cut's small, mean eyes narrow. "Where's your psycho boyfriend? He owes me a shirt. Look at this shit." He tugs his ripped collar.

I back away, but someone shoves me from behind, and I stagger into Crew Cut.

"Guess I'll just have to get my money's worth with you." He laughs and pushes me back. The others titter around me, an unsettling, wild sound.

I catch myself before I fall, square my shoulders, and try to put as much super bitch on my face as possible, but he steps forward.

"You ever had a real man?" Crew Cut asks.

I try to ignore his words, cut off the cold fear that blooms in my stomach. The stench of beer pours from his skin as he steps closer. The road is only a few feet away, but it might as well be miles. I'm the gazelle on those wildlife shows—see how the hyenas surround their prey. I wish I were stronger, faster, anywhere but here.

One of the men lunges at me. I dodge to the side, but there's nowhere to go. Strong arms clamp around me from behind. I scream and try to elbow my captor, but I have no leverage. The arms tighten.

"Shut her up," whispers Crew Cut. He glances nervously at the mostly dark buildings towering over us.

A hand claps over my mouth. I drive the heel of my boot down hard on my captor's toes, and squirming out of my coat, I twist free. I manage a few shambling steps, making it to the wood-plank sidewalk before rough hands seize me again.

I claw blindly, pulling away strips of skin, I don't care whose. I forget about running. I forget everything. All that matters is this. I'll keep clawing until they stop coming.

A fist collides with my face, my nose breaks with a sickening crunch, and I crumple to the pavement, my face a mask of agony. Shaking, I climb to my hands and knees. Blood patters to the sidewalk in garish splotches. Will the morning commuters and mothers with their strollers see this bloody puddle and wonder who it came from? Or will the police scrub away this stain of violence from the civilized world with a ho-hum, how awful, but boys will be boys, all the while thinking *she must have done something to provoke them?*

A foot crashes into my side, and the ground rushes forward. I swing my hand around just in time to avoid a face plant.

"Stupid bitch!" Crew Cut yells. "You scratched the shit outta my arm."

Another foot catches me low in the back. Something cracks inside me, and a hot chill runs up my spine. Then feet fly at me from all directions, and I curl into a ball, covering my head.

After what seems like a long time, the kicking stops. I allow myself a moment's hope and peek out from under my arm.

Crew Cut stands at my feet. He draws a knife from his pocket and pries it open. My blood goes cold.

The other men standing over me stare slack-jawed, their eyes darting between me and the knife in Crew Cut's fist. One steps forward. "Whoa, man. Let's get out of here. She ain't worth it."

"Aw, John, don't be a pussy. A shirt for a shirt's only fair. I just wanna see if she looks any better without clothes."

Grinning, he bends toward me. He bends forever, his face inching closer and closer. I wait, ignoring the pain crawling along my ribs, the realization that I feel nothing past my hips.

My hands fly at him, aiming for his eyes. My fingers tear at his face, and bits of him lodge under my nails. He slashes at my arms, the knife a swinging silver blur. Blood pools in my armpits. His blood? Mine? It has to be mine, but I never felt the blade. It's always like that, it never hurts until I see the yawning cut. Until it's too late, too deep. I smell antiseptic, hear my mother's shrill voice echoing off the walls of the exam room. *What is wrong with you? Why would you do that to yourself?* But I can't say anything: she'd never hear anything against him.

The exam room dissolves into Jamison Square, where Crew Cut is climbing to his feet, clutching his face in one hand. He pins me to the ground with one giant shoe between my breasts. I grab for his leg.

"Try it and I'll crush you," he says, applying pressure.

Blood rolls down the side of his face and drips from his chin. He wipes it away. Three angry red furrows span his cheek. I missed both of his eyes, unfortunately. They gleam in the half-light, and in them I can see he *wants* to crush me. Because he enjoys it, or to mend his wounded pride? Both? It doesn't matter; the result is the same. I hold up my bloody hands in surrender.

For a frightening moment, the pressure increases, and I'm sure my ribs will crack. I imagine them breaking, their broken edges stabbing into my soft tissues. How long can I live with a punctured lung? Three minutes? Ten?

His foot eases off a little, and I take a shallow, aching breath.

"Hold her arms," Crew Cut says.

No one moves. John, the one who spoke up before, stands a little taller, his eyes wide at all the blood. "No, man." The other is shaking his head too, whispering *oh, shit* over and over under his breath. His eyes dart between the buildings, the dead trees, the knife.

Crew Cut laughs and his foot presses down hard, forcing the air from my lungs in a rush. He doesn't notice. "Fuck you guys. Go on, pussies. Run home. But if you nark . . ." He waves his knife at them.

John opens his mouth to say something, his eyes drop to me and he quickly looks away, shaking his head. He and the other guy share a glance, they both nod and take off through the square. Their footfalls are swallowed by darkness. I wish the darkness would take me too. Soon. How much blood have I lost? I resist the urge to look.

Crew Cut's foot lifts from my aching ribs and he drops to his knees and sits astride my hips. The knife trembles a little in his fist, but I don't think it's out of fear. "It's just us now," he says, breathing raggedly.

I try to keep my face impassive as he leans forward, crushing me against the cold pavement. "I'll bet you taste sweet."

His breath is hot on my neck, and I can smell beer and his aftershave—Old Spice. The same kind my father used. I shudder, and the light shifts. Crew Cut's blonde hair lengthens and darkens, and his eyes change. They are no longer mean, swampy pits. They are *his* eyes. Green eyes. My father's eyes.

Dad's eyes were brighter when he drank, and they were always bright when he came for me. I hated their brightness. I hated him. I hated the pungent stench of vodka that rose from his too-hot skin. But part of me loved him, loved that he noticed me. It validated me, proved I existed. Part of me was so starved for his affection, it latched on to anything and sucked it up greedily. Even if it hurt and was confusing, and the wounds were too deep to heal. Even if it killed me inside.

I squeeze my eyes shut, and when I open them again, my father is gone. He was never here, of course; it's Crew Cut on top of me. His weight is unbearable, cutting off my breath. Black dots dance in front of my eyes. I fight the urge to squirm beneath him. Men like him like it when you squirm. Bile burns in the back of my throat.

His mouth finds my ear again. "You're gonna be a good girl and not fight, or I might cut you."

I nod against the rough stubble of his cheek, unable to speak.

"Good."

His weight moves off my chest and air rushes into my lungs, painfully expanding my compressed and battered ribs. His cold blade touches my stomach, and I gasp. It slips under the edge of my corset. Irrationally I want to tell him he can just untie it, to please not ruin my favorite corset, but my throat is too dry for more than a hoarse croak, and my vision is swimming.

The sound of his knife sawing through the thick fabric is somehow more final than the blood, the pain, and I know it's over. There's no getting out of this. I hope I bleed out before he starts. I embrace the darkness encroaching on my vision and retreat into the calm silence there, sinking deeper, detaching from everything. The pain, the fear, it's all still there, only muted—numb. It belongs to some other girl. A blade nicks that girl's skin, and a warm wetness blooms and dribbles down her side as she stares unseeing at the indifferent stars above.

Someone once said never wish upon a star because the stars are just ghosts. They shine bright and hopeful above, but in the time it has taken for their shimmering light to reach Earth, they have long since burnt out. They are dead, just like our dreams.

Deep inside my shell, I wish to join them.

Chapter 3

Everything is red, like fire, burning. I'm dying. My blood is acid, creeping, searing, eating me from the inside out. I try to scream. I am screaming. A voice, soothing in the dark, whispers something, then it's blotted out by pain. Blackness engulfs me.

❖ ❖ ❖

I wake with a shriek and clutch at the blankets surrounding me. I'm on a huge bed. Whose bed? Where? Images swim in my mind. Skeletal trees, a red brick fountain in the darkness. I smell the ghost of summer chlorine. It's so vivid, I can't be sure if this bed is a dream, and I'm really somewhere else.

Jamison Square?

I shut my eyes, and the images intensify. Men's faces. A flash of silver—a blade. Blood.

My eyes snap open, and I push back the long sleeves of my oversized black shirt—whose shirt? I find nothing, no cuts, no blood. I should feel relieved, but panic blooms instead. How long have I been here? My vision wavers, darkens. Three men tower over me, wet smiles on their hungry faces. Did one of them take me to their house? Was it all a dream?

The bedroom is large and sparsely furnished. Just the bed, two side tables, and a simple wooden chair. A row of enormous windows spans the wall to my left. In front of me, two ancient-looking tapestries flank a door of dark wood—real wood too, from the looks of it, not the flimsy hollow kind. The tapestries must have been vibrant once, deep burgundy and gold, but whatever scenes they portrayed have faded beyond recognition. It's an odd decor choice for the dumb jock type. Maybe he lives with his parents? No shock there.

I throw back the covers to find I'm wearing a god-awful pair of men's neon green jogging shorts. My skin is blindingly white in comparison, and I'm reminded of the time Lisa talked me into that bikini contest. Me in combat boots and a Day-Glo orange bikini—Lisa's decision, not mine—popping balloons with my ass for a crowd of drunk men. We all have regrets.

But, where are my clothes? Do I want to know? That's a dumb question—of course I do. I think. I hold my breath, lift my shirt, and pull out the waist of my shorts. My breath releases at the sight of my ratty old underwear. The fact that they're still on and in the same, somewhat delicate, condition is a good sign. But at the same time, how long have I been wearing them? Worries for another time.

I slide from the bed, shivering as my bare toes touch the cold wood floor. Muted grey light dribbles in from the windows. Is it morning? Afternoon? It's hard to tell in the rainy season. I creep to the windows, relieved that the floor doesn't creak, and I peer out. It's a straight drop to sharp gravel, two stories at least. Maybe I could tie the bed sheets? They're always doing that in movies.

I'm considering jumping anyway when I hear muffled footsteps from behind the door. My eyes dart around the room, coming to rest on the chair. I could hit them with it. I could hide. There are two other doors in the room. Bathroom? Closet? Exit? I stand there forever, my eyes bouncing from the chair, the windows, the doors. The footsteps are closer now, but I can hardly hear them over the racket of my thrashing heart.

A gentle knock breaks my paralysis. I dive for the bed and yank the covers over my head, huddling beneath like a child, as if the knocking at the door is a monster that can be repelled through will alone. Mom used to say monsters couldn't get you if you hid under the covers. Too bad that never works on the human kind.

I hold my breath, hoping whoever it is will go away, but the door swings open. I peek over the comforter to see a tall man with long dark hair standing in the doorway. He's casually dressed in black jeans and a plain black t-shirt. His mouth is turned down just slightly at the corners, giving him a brooding, serious look. I stifle a gasp.

"Sasha?"

My name sounds strange on his lips. I didn't imagine him, and he's even more beautiful than I remember. I lower the covers slightly but say nothing. I can't trust my mouth to form a coherent sentence. I peer past him into what I assume is a hallway, but he's alone.

"It's good to see you're awake. I was beginning to worry I'd done it wrong. I'm sure you're confused." He starts forward, and I shrink back, lifting my blanket barrier.

"Did what wrong? What happened? How did I get here? Where am I?"

He cocks his head. "You don't remember? You took a pretty bad beating. I dealt with the men responsible and brought you here."

"Beating? Men?" It definitely wasn't a dream, but then how . . . I resist the urge to examine myself again as laughter and harsh voices echo in my mind. Now I remember, not everything, but enough. "What do you mean, you dealt with them?"

His eyes blaze. "They won't harm anyone again."

Oh my god, he killed them. I knew he was nuts. Those men deserved to die, and part of me hopes he made them suffer— but at the same time, what kind of person could kill three people? A psychopath, that's who. But . . . *them*? It had only been only one in the end. How did he find the others? I picture him stalking them in the dark, hunting them, slaughtering them. Tension creeps into my shoulders. How long before he decides I should be killed too? "How'd you do it?" I ask. I should at least know what I'm getting into, right?

"There's much to discuss. I'll explain all I can, but first—" He takes a step toward the bed, and I jerk away. My back slams into the headboard. It's bare wood and it should hurt, but I hardly feel it.

He flinches as if I hit him, and his stupid-beautiful face creases with concern. I know psychopaths don't feel emotion, so he's obviously a great actor.

"I won't hurt you."

I gape at him. I bet that's what he said to those men before he killed them. "Were you following me?" An accusatory tone creeps into my voice. I don't want him to think I'm ungrateful—he's likely saved my life—but the creep factor is high. How long had he watched before deciding to step in?

He's quiet for a moment, as if debating how much to say. "I followed them to the club. I should have left when they did, but—"

"Why were you following them? Are you a stalker?"

His eyes drop to his hands and he shakes his head. "It doesn't matter. You wouldn't believe me if I told you. This is my fault. I know nothing can make what they did, what I do, I mean *did* right, but I had to."

Alarms are blaring in my head, insisting that I shut up now, but words come out of my mouth anyway. "You didn't have to . . ." I regain enough sense to stop short of saying the words *kill* or *murder* as if speaking them might awaken his bloodlust and I feel my lip curl in disgust. I've become just like my mother, tiptoeing around Dad's trigger words. My anger swells, filling my chest until I'm afraid I'll burst. "You could have . . . I don't know, maybe . . . called the police?" With each word my voice grows higher. I'm near hysterics. Soon only dogs will be able to hear me.

He huffs, and a sneer twitches his mouth. "The police take far too long. My justice is swift."

"Your *justice*?" Jesus. He *is* crazy; it's always the pretty ones. Now it's words like *serial killer*, *sociopath*, and *psychotic* that swirl in my head. I shouldn't provoke him, but I can't stop myself. "What are you, some sort of vigilante?"

He shrugs. "The police couldn't have helped. When I found you, you had gone into shock. You suffered severe blood loss."

"Did he . . . Was I . . ." My mouth works, but the word won't come out, as if saying it will make it real. I can almost feel Crew Cut's grabbing hands, his breath against my neck, his cold blade. I suppress a shiver and clamp my arms around my chest. My throat tightens.

Ambrose grimaces. "Raped?"

I nod, swallowing hard against the lump in my throat.

His jaw clenches. I can tell he wants to look away, but he holds my eyes, shakes his head. His mouth moves, but there's no sound. He tries again, louder. "No."

I watch his face, not sure if I can trust him. He could have raped me himself for all I know. I wonder if he's lying, but realize I don't want to know. I've been holding my breath, and now I release it in a sigh. Some of the tension eases from my shoulders.

"How are you feeling?" His voice is soothing, and concern creases his brow. He starts to take a step toward the bed but stops.

What a stupid question. "Shouldn't I have bruises, cuts . . . broken bones?"

He nods slowly, as if considering what to say. "They've healed."

I feel the blood drain from my face. Maybe it's been weeks; he's kept me here locked up, drugged up while my injuries healed. My hands want to shake; I ball them into hard fists against my sides. He doesn't look crazy, but there's no doubt as to what he is, what I am. I read *Misery*. This will end badly.

He frowns and takes a half step closer. "Are you all right?"

My heart skitters and I slam into the headboard again. Damn it, my only chance of getting out of this is to act normal. I take a deep breath and smile at him. It feels fake. It is fake.

His frown deepens. "There's no need to fear me. I won't harm you. Is there anything I can say to put you at ease?"

You're free to leave comes to mind, but I'm not about to say that. "Where am I?"

"My house. I brought you here Friday night. Early Saturday morning to be exact. It's Tuesday now."

Tuesday? He's obviously lying—wounds can't heal that fast. I can feel his eyes on me as I try to work it out. "Why? Why not take me to a hospital?"

His face is calm and serious as he shakes his head. "You were beyond the help of doctors. Normally you would have been eased in, given a choice, but you were unconscious and losing far too much blood. If I hadn't changed you, you would have died. We call it Cnila Hom."

"Wait. A choice? Changed? Key-nala what?"

He holds up his hand and takes a cautious step forward. "Cnila Hom. Loosely translated, it means bloodlife."

"Translated from what? Martian?"

He gives a little shrug, or maybe it's a wince. Whatever it is, it doesn't quite look like a denial. I'd meant it as a joke, and I almost laugh. I *want* to laugh, but I've watched enough movies to know not to laugh in the face of a serial killer, especially not one this delusional. He's a whole new level of crazy. But hey, maybe I won't be hobbled. Instead I'll be forced to do who knows what with some X-Files blood freak.

"If it's proof you need," he says, "look at your arms. They were covered with cuts, and now there's not so much as a scar."

I know there are no cuts, and now that he mentions it, I hadn't seen scars either. I push back my sleeves again. My arms are smooth, pristine. Even the gridwork of self-inflicted scars—the road map of my angst-ridden youth—is gone.

I tug my right sleeve farther up and raise my arm overhead. The chicken pox scar on the inside of my upper arm has vanished too. Something weird is going on. I need time to think. But I need to get out of here first, and sooner would be better.

He pushes his hair from his face. "Say something."

"What do you want from me?" I can't trust my voice above a whisper. I clench my fists to hold back my tears.

His eyes meet mine and they are so strange, so beautiful. "Nothing." He stuffs his hands into the pockets of his jeans. "You must think I'm insane, and I don't blame you. Please. Allow me the rest of the day to convince you." His gaze shifts away before returning. "Then, if you still don't believe me, you're free to go."

I want to believe him. His face is sincere and he doesn't look crazy. But despite what I'd like to believe, I've never been a good judge of character. "You'd let me leave?"

"Of course!" His eyebrows bunch together and his voice softens. "Do you truly think so ill of me?"

"I don't know what to think. I just woke up here . . ." I glare at him, my fingers digging into the comforter. "Where are my clothes?"

He holds my gaze. "They were ruined."

I clutch the blankets over my chest.

"I'm hardly the sort to ogle a battered woman." He crosses to the door by the windows and steps inside, returning a moment later with my boots and a stack of neatly folded clothes.

"These should do for now." He points to the door on the opposite side of the room. "There's a restroom just through there. I'll be down in the library, just to the right of the stairs; join me when you're ready." He exits into the hall and pulls the door closed behind him.

His footsteps recede, and when I'm sure he's gone, I throw the covers back and sit up. My head aches. I want to believe he's sane, that he's only helping. But he just admitted to killing three people. True, they were disgusting jerks, and sure, I'm kind of happy they're dead—but he's still a murderer.

I massage my temples and stare out the window at the grey sky. Nothing good could ever come of getting involved with this man, and I can't trust myself to make smart decisions—not around him. I need to leave now.

I untangle myself from the blankets and walk to the chair, eyeing the clothes piled there: A pair of jeans and a fresh long-sleeved shirt, almost exactly like the one I'm wearing, including the fact that it's several sizes too large. It's probably his. I hold the jeans to my waist. These, at least, will fit. Who knows where he got them. I don't want to know. At least they're black.

I bring the shirt to my face, and before I realize what I'm doing, my eyes close and I'm breathing it in. It smells clean with a hint of spice—clove? I remember the soft brush of his lips against my hand, and my cheeks burn. I need to get out of here. I dress, give the bathroom door a forlorn look—a shower would be great—and head for the door.

I step out into a dim hallway. To the left, a glass door leads out onto a tiny terrace, and to the right, past a wide staircase, is a closed door, another room? There's no time to explore; I creep down the stairs, luckily the steps are stone, so they won't creak, but still I place each foot softly.

The stairs flow into a circular foyer lined with doors, all of them closed except the first on the right, where I assume he waits, but I don't approach it. Instead I focus on the door that looks the most like a front door—wide and more ornate than the others. I sneak closer, my boots barely a whisper on the tile.

I reach for the knob, and my hand shakes. It'll be locked, impossible to open from the inside—but the knob turns freely. I hold my breath and pull, gritting my teeth against the inevitable squeal of hinges, but the door swings open smoothly, silently, and I step out onto the front porch. Fresh air greets me, cold and slatey with the promise of rain. It has never smelled so good.

My legs feel powerful as I take off down the driveway. I run, wildly, blindly pushing myself faster. With each stride I'm sure footsteps follow, but I don't dare look back. And as I run, the rain comes, falling in torrential sheets.

Chapter 4

I don't stop until I reach my apartment complex. I've never run so long or so far in my life. Seven, eight miles? I vaguely remember crossing a bridge, maybe Burnside? It's all a blur, but somehow I managed it and I'm not even out of breath. It actually feels weird to not be running, like my legs are made of over-stretched rubber bands.

Water drips from my hair and face, and my shirt is slicked to my chest. At least I'm wearing my good boots—the ones that don't have holes in the soles—so my feet are dry. And thankfully, the pro-life protesters are elsewhere today. They're usually only out when it's nice out, screaming on their bullhorns at eight in the morning while the civilized world tries to sleep. I guess life doesn't matter in inclement weather.

I climb the steps to the back entrance, fumbling for my keys. I can't wait to get in, take a shower, put on some fresh clothes—my own clothes—make some hot cocoa . . . my keys! I pat my pockets again, sure I've missed something, but then I remember: they were in my coat pocket. Where's my coat? Probably still with psycho. Great. I'll have to talk to the manager, who's almost never in her office. I cross my fingers and walk around to the front.

It's my lucky day. The office door stands open, perhaps for the first time in two years, and the manager is in. She's a useless woman who loses rent checks and forgets maintenance requests, but she hands over a spare key without so much as a raised eyebrow at my disheveled appearance, and in that moment I love her, vacant eyes and all.

❖ ❖ ❖

I've never been happier to see my boring little studio. It's cramped and messy, but blissfully psycho-free. I pause in the kitchen to peel off my soaked and dripping clothes, toss them in the sink on top of a cluster of tea mugs, and streak to the bathroom.

I'm just shutting the door when a loud honking buzz issues from my room. Yanking a towel from its hook, I peer around the door. My phone is ringing on the nightstand next to my lumpy futon. Its lights flash as it spins in lazy circles, arcing closer and closer to the edge.

My bare feet slap across the cold wood and I catch the phone before it tumbles to the ground. It hums in my hand like a living thing. I don't recognize the number, but I'm sure it's him. My chest tightens. I imagine his perfect lips and his strange eyes. I want to answer and tell him I'm sorry for leaving, that I don't care how crazy he is, we can make it work so long as he promises not to kill me next.

Instead I drop the phone back to the table like it sprouted barbs. How disgustingly shallow can I be? I did the right thing in getting away. I won't be Bonnie to his Clyde. I prefer a quiet life without madness and police chases, thanks.

I watch the phone until it falls silent. A moment later it chimes, announcing voicemail. I snatch it off the table, nearly toppling a mug off the nightstand. I should really pick up some of this mess. I activate the screen, and to my surprise, my phone's calendar display reveals it really is Tuesday, and still February at that. Part of me, the crazy part, screams, *See, he wasn't lying!*

Five missed calls and three texts? Suddenly I'm popular. I dial voicemail and gag as I get an earful of Rick's sleazy faux concern. He can't understand why I just quit. He wants to discuss what went wrong. I roll my eyes. "Your hands are what went wrong, jerk." I punch the pound sign and skip to the next message.

Lisa's jubilant voice pours from the speaker. She can't believe I'm still sleeping, it's past two. She wants to know all about the handsome man I was talking to, and if I went home with him.

I groan and stab the pound sign.

"It's Lisa. Again . . . Remember me? Yeah, call when you two stop sucking face—"

Pound.

Lisa again. "Where are you? I stopped by your place last night and there was no answer. Seriously, call me . . . text, whatever. I just want to make sure you're still alive."

There's a moment of silence as the message ends and the next begins. Ambrose's voice issues from the speaker, and my cheeks grow warm. "I know I've frightened you, but I must speak with you. Please call."

The phone tumbles from my hand. It's scary how rational he sounds, how normal. I bet that's what everyone thought about that Jim Jones guy too, and look where it got them.

My eyes fall to my wallet lying open beside the phone. There's an empty space where my ID usually sits. I suck in a breath. My ID was in my coat too. He has it now, probably in a drawer full of IDs. I imagine him rifling through them, remembering his past victims. Wait. If he has my ID, he knows where I live. He could be on his way right now.

Cursing, I dash to the closet, tug on a fresh t-shirt and jeans, and jerk a hoodie over my head. I rip my travel bag from the top shelf, the side pocket fat with a few months-worth of saved tips, and toss in a few changes of clothes, resisting the urge to look over my shoulder at the door. At any moment, I expect to hear the lock turn, the scuff of the door sweeping over the entry mat.

I fling my bag on the bed and scoop my phone, its charger, and my wallet inside, then spin around trying to see everything at once: the plain, oppressively white cinderblock walls, books everywhere in leaning stacks, spilling from overstuffed shelves. When did all this stuff get so out of control? My eyes flit from stack to stack. It feels like I'm forgetting something, but running always feels like that.

I zip the bag, flip up my hood, and grab my umbrella from the corner by the door. A quick peek through the spyhole reveals a deserted hallway, pukey green carpet, white brick, flickering fluorescents. I lock the door behind me and head back out into the downpour.

❖ ❖ ❖

I find myself across the street from the coffee shop where I wasted six months of my life. Rain patters on my umbrella, each drop progressively louder, pounding. A headache too? Just when I thought this day couldn't get any worse.

Through the dirty glass storefront, I glimpse Lisa behind the counter, but I can't see anyone else, not even customers—big surprise there. Two cars are parked out front, and thankfully, neither belongs to Rick. I heave a sigh and splash across the street.

The bell over the door clangs—loud and brain-piercingly horrible, and Lisa looks over her shoulder. Her jaw falls open and she nearly drops a stack of coffee mugs. "Where the hell have you been?"

"I don't want to talk about it. Not here." My voice sounds steadier than I feel.

She gives me a testy glare, noisily stacking an armload of mugs on the counter. The clatter of porcelain makes my ears bleed.

"It's just us—Dana's in the back doing dishes." She starts to grab another stack of mugs, but freezes. Her voice lowers. "Was it that guy?"

I can feel her examining me, but I can't look at her—her eyes are too probing. She'll get the truth out of me, and then I'll start crying. I focus on the floor and swallow hard.

"That jerk! Are you okay? What di—"

"I'm fine. I don't want to talk about it." I can feel her eyes on my face again, but I keep my gaze fixed on the tile.

She rushes around the counter and stops short, eyeing my bag. "Going somewhere?"

"I need a place to stay. Would you mind?"

She bites her lip. "Dave's coming over tonight."

"Seriously? Come on! I can't go home right now. I have nowhere else. You know I can't afford a hotel. Tell Dave you're busy."

Her face goes blank, in a creepy, *Twilight Zone* kind of way, and a soft sigh falls from her lips. "I'll tell Dave I'm busy." Her voice sounds flat, soft, almost monotone, and her eyes have a vacant look like someone pulled the plug that connects her brain.

"Uh, hello?" I wave my hand in front of her face. "So you're not seeing Dave tonight?"

Her eyes flutter and her forehead scrunches. "I just told you, I'm going to tell him I'm busy." She does that cocker spaniel head tilt, one hand on her hip. "You sure you're okay? You're acting really weird."

Oh, yeah, I'm acting weird? I want to squeeze my pounding head. "Never mind. So I can stay with you?"

"Yeah, sure, but I want to hear everything. I'm stuck here until five, but you can head over if you want. The door's never locked."

"You're freaked out about people disappearing, but you don't lock your doors? That makes no sense."

"Someone's always home." She shrugs and makes her way back to the counter. "You could hang here a bit. It's dead." She plucks a mug from the top of the espresso machine. "Latte on Rick?"

I wrinkle my nose.

"Sorry, I forgot. Hot chocolate? Chai?"

Not even an hour ago hot chocolate sounded wonderful, but now the thought makes me want to gag. What's wrong with me? "No. I just need some rest."

Lisa sighs, roughly returns the mug. "Kay, be boring. See ya."

Chapter 5

I only get lost once on my way to Lisa's house, which is pretty good for me. I've been over many times so I don't have an excuse, I'm just directionally challenged. It's quite fitting really.

I open the door and peer in, feeling like a criminal. The stench of pot and dog piss-soaked carpet assaults my senses. They don't even have a dog, it's just the lingering scent of dog pisses past. I hold my breath and follow the stained carpet through to the dingy but surprisingly clean kitchen.

Handwritten signs cling to nearly every surface. One demands the reader clean up after themselves because "your mom doesn't live here." Another is a reminder that rent is due by the first, "NO exceptions!" "No" is underlined three times; the sign means business. On the fridge, some intellectual genius has arranged a swarm of word magnets to read, "moldy heteroflexible cave perhaps naked bounty." Whatever that means.

For half a second I consider raiding the medicine cabinet for Tylenol, but it's too much effort. Sleep will help. I climb the stairs and seal myself in Lisa's room. It's cleaner than the rest of the house and smells much better. Grey day leaks in around the heavy black drapes. Perfect sleeping conditions. The shower, and everything else, can wait.

I drop my bag by the door and stretch out on her bed, a real bed, a billion times better than my lumpy futon. My eyes shut and I'm in the park again. A silver blade flashes in the dark and bites into my palm. A man laughs. My eyes snap open, and I spread my hands before my face—unmarked.

"I just want to sleep," I whisper to the room, like a prayer. My head aches—my whole body aches. I stare at the ceiling, picking out patterns in the off-white plateaus and craters, the constellations of urban life. They foretell nothing great.

At some point I must have slept because the light from the window has faded and I feel a little better. I can probably handle a shower. I stand, and the room revolves around me. I grope for the dresser to keep from crashing to the floor. Suddenly I realize what I'm feeling. When did I last eat? Did he feed me? I shove the thought away. I don't even want to think about how he would have fed me. Visions of funnels and feeding tubes and IVs dance in my mind. Could he possibly be that crazy?

Another wave of vertigo washes over me, and I clutch the dresser again. My headache is back with a vengeance, but this is a problem I can solve. I work my way down to the kitchen, moving like an old woman on her sixth hip replacement. At last, I make it to the fridge with its promise of naked bounty. False advertising. The only bounty it holds is prehistoric condiments, some cheap beer, and a crusty jug of milk—closer to cheese by now.

I let the door close with a grunt and notice half a loaf of unsliced bread on the counter with a note: "Lisa's—DON'T TOUCH!" It looks a little stale, but it's not moldy. I cut off a piece with a knife from the crappy knife block on the counter. My stomach grumbles, and I stuff the entire slice in my mouth, chewing greedily. It tastes awful, like musty cardboard, but I keep at it anyway, chewing and swallowing. It'll make me feel better, I hope; I'll find something tastier later. Right now I just have to make the spinning stop.

I choke down another piece and I'm going for a third when the knife slips. I curse even though it doesn't hurt. It never does, not until the blood starts. There's nothing at first, just a pale slit, but then the blood wells up, and a moment later, stinging, throbbing pain. I rush to the bathroom, wrap a wad of toilet paper around the cut, and rip open the medicine cabinet. No Band-Aids, no ointments, no pain meds either—the cabinet is barren. Who lives like this?

Before I can move on to cursing Lisa and her obviously inhuman roommates, my stomach emits a loud whining gurgle and I double over. My lips grow cold and a hot stabbing pain races up my spine. My legs buckle, and I collapse in front of the toilet. The stench of urine is so strong my stomach heaves, and I barely manage to flip up the lid before everything comes back up.

Too much, too soon. I stand, my knees shaking, and drink a handful of water from the tap. The cool liquid feels good on my throat, and I swallow another handful. My stomach jerks, and I'm puking again. My skin prickles hot and cold, and I rise shakily. "What the hell is going on?" I whisper, my voice raw.

I recover enough to stand, and I swing the medicine cabinet shut. My reflection jumps out at me: sickly pale, dark smudges beneath my eyes. I step closer to the mirror and gasp. My eyes, usually dark green, are violet. The same shade as Ambrose's. I back away and nearly tumble into the tub, narrowly saving myself with the shower curtain, which miraculously doesn't tear.

Pull yourself together. It's just contacts, don't be so stupid! Leaning into the mirror, I run a finger over my eye. There's nothing there, only the wetness of my eyeball. I blink and scrub at my eyes, but nothing changes.

I bolt from the bathroom and crash into one of Lisa's roommates. We tumble to the floor in a jumble of limbs, and I come down hard on his chest, our foreheads knock together.

"Ah! Jesus!" he yells.

"Sorry." I try to push myself off him, my arms shaking. My stomach growls—Oh god. Please don't puke—but it's not that kind of growl, and for a moment my eyes fix on his neck. I'm hypnotized by the rapid pulsing beneath his skin. I roll off him, shouting "Sorry!" I can't seem to say anything else as I scramble up the stairs.

I slam Lisa's door behind me, and a ragged laugh-sob escapes my throat. What the fuck was that? All I can hear over the pounding in my ears is Ambrose's voice repeating over and over: *bloodlife*.

Blood.

I can't breathe. Each breath is like sucking mud through a fine straw. What's happening to me? I lean against the door, head between my knees, taking slow wheezing breaths, until at last, my chest loosens.

Downstairs, the front door opens, muffled conversation floats up, then feet clump up the stairs. I scoot away from the door and hug my knees, trying to cradle both my throbbing toilet paper-wrapped finger and my pounding head. The door opens, and Lisa spots me on the floor. I'm sure I look like a psych patient. I'm even rocking back and forth. I force myself to sit still.

"Hey, you okay?" Lisa hooks her thumb over her shoulder. "Rob was just saying you ran into him super hard. You freaked him out."

I shrug without looking up, keeping my face against my palms. "Yeah, fine."

"You don't look so good. You're kinda pale." She laughs. "I mean, more than usual. Come on. What's up?"

She tugs my elbow until I stand and leads me to her bed. The mattress dips as she settles down beside me.

"Tell me what's wrong. Where have you been? I called and texted." The concern in her voice is real. I never thought she cared—but then I guess it's my own fault for never opening up to her. Never trusting her, or anyone, with the real me.

I focus on my hands; my bandaged finger itches horribly, and I ball my fist to keep from scratching it to shreds. I don't know where to start—it all sounds so crazy. "I almost died after Vox . . . or maybe I did. I don't really know."

Her jaw drops and she leans closer. "What? How? Were you in the hospital? Wait, what do you mean you don't know?"

"These guys jumped me and . . . that guy, Ambrose, the one from Vox, he helped me, or he says he did. He said—I don't know. I just woke up at his house. He said . . ." My voice cracks and my throat closes. The room spins. I think I'm going to be sick again.

Her hands are on my shoulders, her face hovers directly in front of mine. I don't look up. "He said what?"

I take a deep breath, still refusing to meet her eyes. "He killed them."

"Holy—" She sucks in a breath and finally draws back, releasing me. "Seriously? He actually told you he killed them?"

"Well, he didn't use those words exactly. I don't know. He said a bunch of crazy shit."

"Crazier than killing people?"

I nod. "I feel stupid even saying this but—" I look down at my hand; the cut on my finger has stopped throbbing. I peel off the toilet paper. My finger is smeared with dried blood, but the cut is gone, not just healed, gone. "Huh . . ."

"What?"

I leap to my feet. "I have to go."

"Go?" She springs from the bed and seizes my shoulders. "Go where? What's going—Oh my god! Your eyes!"

Her voice is like an icepick straight into my brain. I wince and shift back, but she steps closer for a better look. Then I can smell her. Coffee and fallen leaves, and another, deeper smell that I can't place. Something I need. My mouth waters, and distantly, I realize my pain is gone. My vision pulses with the softly thrumming artery in her neck.

I catch her in my arms and squeeze—hard. She stiffens against me and tries to squirm free, but I'm stronger. Much stronger. Her struggles awaken something predatory in me— the thrashing mouse beneath the cat's paw—and my arms tighten, drawing her closer.

"Ow! Stop."

Her voice is a whisper, nearly inaudible over the pounding of her heart—my heart? So loud. And beneath that, a softer, sighing sound, like a swift moving stream under thick ice. My eyes close and my lips brush her neck. This feels right.

She screams, high and grating, drowning out the soft river and the heavy pounding. My eyes pop open and I see her, wide-eyed, shaking, fragile. I gasp and pull away. What the hell am I doing?

I grab my bag and flee.

❖ ❖ ❖

A mile or so later, the adrenaline fades and the dizziness creeps back in. The throbbing behind my eyes is worse than ever. As an added bonus, I'm soaked again, having forgotten my umbrella at Lisa's, and the rain has leaked in around my boot laces. So much for good soles.

I duck into the first public place I see, a dingy red and black dive bar called King's Tavern. Rock music pounds from the speakers at an unbearable level. I order a lemon drop from the jaded bartender, who rolls her eyes, but thankfully, doesn't bother asking for my ID—it's the bags under my eyes, probably—and I slide into a high-backed booth farthest from the blaring speakers.

My drink stinks of rubbing alcohol with a dash of furniture polish, and I push it away. I've puked enough for one day, besides, I only bought it so I could sit in peace without feeling guilty. I shut my eyes against the spinning, and Lisa's face floats up in the darkness.

I fish my phone from my bag and bring up her name on a message screen. The cursor blinks, waiting. What can I possibly say to fix this? *Sorry I tried to eat you?* Maybe a joke about long pig? I slam the phone on the table and massage my temples. Lisa's the closest thing I've had to a friend since—well, since ever, and I fucked it up.

There's only one option. I have to talk to him. I need to know what's going on. I take a deep breath, and dial the first number under missed calls.

Ambrose answers on the first ring—as if he was waiting for me. He knew I'd call. I'd have to sooner or later. It makes me sick, needing something from him. He has power over me, knowledge, and he can use it to control me. I shut my eyes and try to silence my thoughts.

"Can we still talk?" My stomach bunches into knots. I'm going to be sick again.

❋ ❋ ❋

I watch the door, shrinking in my seat every time it opens. Was calling him the right decision? So much has happened that's beyond explanation in a rational world. I wanted to tear into Lisa's neck. There's no rational explanation for that.

The door opens, and it's Ambrose. My heart races, and I quickly look away, pretending to be engrossed in my phone. I hope it's too dark for him to notice how my hands shake.

"You're here. I half expected you to be gone."

I glance up from my phone, and my mouth falls open. He looks perfect. I feel disgusting in comparison, like a drowned rat. I resist the urge to flip up my hood, and I give him a soggy smile.

"You left this earlier." He holds my coat out—a peace offering.

I take it and surreptitiously slip my hand into the pocket. My keys and ID are still there, along with a stick of eyeliner. I'll be needing that last item; I look like a troll.

He's watching me, and I expect him to be angry or disappointed, but he looks relieved. Maybe he really is just trying to help. "You can sit if you want."

He nods and slips in across from me, folding his hands on the table. "Thank you for calling. I've been worried about you." His voice lowers and I strain to hear him over the music. "You haven't killed anyone, have you?"

I glare at him through my limp, dripping hair. He's the serial killer, not me. I try to keep the look of horror off my face, but he winces.

His shoulders relax slightly. "No. I can see you haven't."

What's that supposed to mean? I want to ask but he's already moving on.

"I understand why you ran. You didn't choose this, and perhaps it was selfish of me to force it on you, but I couldn't let you die." His hair falls over his eyes as he studies his hands, and he's quiet for a moment. "I've never done this before, and I fear I've made an awful mess. I usually make a point of avoiding hu—people. I should have stayed on those men when they left. It's my fault they hurt you. If I would have just done what I set out to do." He looks away, blushing slightly. "I'm sorry."

The look on his face is so tragic, I want to cry. I want to reach across the table, take his hands in mine, and tell him it's okay, that I'm glad he helped, I'm glad he talked to me, I'm glad he's here. Anything to get that look off his face. But my voice won't work, and my hands might as well be glued to the table in front of me. I swallow hard and take a deep breath. "Thank you."

His eyes lock on mine and his eyebrows knit together as if he's trying to decipher a hidden message in my words.

"I know you're trying to help. In the last few hours I've . . . well, I've seen some things I can't explain. Scary things."

He nods. "I'm sorry you had to face this alone, but I'm glad for the chance to put it right."

There's an implied *none of this would have been an issue if you hadn't run off.* Or maybe I'm projecting; he doesn't seem like the passive-aggressive type. Still, I can't help feeling a slight pang of guilt, and maybe it shows on my face because his eyes cut away and an awkward silence spreads between us.

He glances at my drink and his mouth quirks down at one corner. "You didn't drink that, did you?"

My stomach does a little flip at the thought, and I shake my head. "I can't keep anything down. I think something's wrong."

He leans forward again, his hands sliding within inches of my own. "Not wrong, just different." His voice lowers again.

"I'm sure you've noticed the changes. Your eyes, teeth . . . cravings?"

My teeth too? I raise a finger to my mouth.

"Careful. They're sharp."

I try to hold my hand steady as I rub one finger along the edge of my teeth. There's an immediate sting, and I jump, jerking my finger from my mouth with a squeak. Ambrose jumps too, as if I've surprised him. Blood beads up and I reach for the napkin underneath my glass, but his fingers close on my wrist. He's gentle, but panic swells in my chest—panic at the way his touch makes my skin burn, panic at the immense strength I sense in him, just below the surface.

He turns my palm toward me and holds my bloody finger in front of my eyes. He wipes the blood away with his thumb, and I freeze in his grasp as the cut, itching and tingling, slowly knits together. It's an odd thing to see.

"What . . ." My voice wavers. "What have you done to me?"

He scans the room. The bar is filling. "This isn't the best place for this conversation."

My shoulders tense. Is he trying to lure me out? Get me alone again? "Where would you rather go?" I tell myself I'm only interested for the sake of sorting this out, not because I love the way he looks or the fluttery feeling I get when I'm near him.

"I'm parked out front. We don't have to go anywhere, just talk in the car."

"You're not trying to kill me?" The words just slip out. I blame the pain, exhaustion, fear. I can't think clearly.

His eyebrows shoot up and his eyes widen comically. "Why would I go through all this trouble just to kill you? I just want to explain everything. I want to help."

Or because you're a psycho? Thankfully, I keep my mouth shut this time, and I study his face, searching for a lie. If he is lying, he's the best liar in the world. There's not so much as an eye twitch. "Okay, I'll listen."

I hope I'm not making a mistake.

Chapter 6

A black van swerves into a mostly deserted parking lot, stopping beneath a grimy sign for King's Tavern. The blonde woman in the driver's seat consults a palm-sized electronic screen where a red light flashes franticly. Rain drums on top of the van as she glances across the cab and out the passenger window—her violet eyes sweep the lot, zeroing in on the bar at its center. The lot seems far too large for such a quiet, rundown place.

She looks back down at the device, at the blinking light, and a crease forms along her forehead. She mutters something in a strange language, and in response, the screen goes dark. When the screen brightens again, the blinking light is gone. Her mouth turns down, but she nods as if this is what she expects, as if this makes sense: the light should've never been there in the first place. She sets the device on the passenger seat, but as she puts the transmission in drive, the light returns, urgently blinking.

The crease in her forehead is back, deeper; if she had eyebrows they would betray her confusion, but there's also, at the corner of her mouth, the hint of a smile, and her eyes gleam in a hopeful, hungry way that's not at all comforting. She places the device in the seat again, gingerly, as if she's afraid to jostle it or look away, as if the blinking light might be a fluke after all, but it continues to flash, strong, brilliant pulses.

She shuts off the engine and retrieves the device, after speaking a few commands, she pauses, her eyes drift back to the shabby red and black building. The screen in her hands appears to be waiting, glowing softly. A minute passes, then her face changes, her chin juts out, head cocked. She removes the key from the ignition and tucks the device into her robe.

The rain stops as she steps from the van, smoothing her hood over her matted blonde hair, eyes fastened across the lot on the battered door beneath the flickering Pabst sign. A clatter of shattering glass draws her attention to the side of the building where a rumpled old man rummages through the refuse tossing bottles and cans into a shopping cart. Her hands form fists within the long sleeves of her robe and a murderous glint steels her eyes, but she forces her palms open and focuses on the bar once more.

A black SUV pulls into the parking lot and the woman watches as the driver parks, only two spaces away even though the lot holds only one other vehicle. The driver, male with long dark hair steps out, his gaze casually sweeps the lot, slipping over the hooded woman and cargo van. His eyes are violet, the same as hers, and she freezes mid-stride, shrinking into her hood. If he noticed her, he shows no sign; he swiftly crosses the lot, hesitates at the door, then there's a swell of music as he slips in.

The woman stares after him, her hand has slipped into her robe where she clutches the screen in her pocket. She takes a faltering step toward the bar, then with a subtle shake of her head, returns to the van. As she climbs into her seat, the rain starts again, harder, pounding on the roof. She watches the door.

Nearly twenty minutes pass, the rain lets up. The man is still inside, and the lot is filling up. Her lip curls and she twists the key in the ignition. Just then, the bar door swings open, and the long-haired man emerges. She perks up in her seat then sags when her eyes land on the woman following behind him. She's wearing a long black coat, running her hands through her damp hair.

She shifts in her seat and consults the screen: the red light is on the move and heading this way. In the shadow of her hood, her nostrils flare, her free hand clutches the steering wheel. She rams the van into drive, and her foot lifts off the brake only to mash back down. Her mouth falls open as the wet-haired woman looks up. Just a brief glance, but there's no missing the flash of violet. Open-mouthed shock dissolves and her lips stretch into a crooked, satisfied grin. Tossing the screen back into the passenger's seat, she lets up off the brake and guides the van out of the lot.

❖ ❖ ❖

The rain is taking a breather as I follow Ambrose across the parking lot. My hair's a soggy mess. I tell myself it doesn't matter, I don't care, even as I rake my fingers through the worst of the tangles. I look up at the sound of an engine from the corner of the lot where some weirdo in a van—wearing what looks like a monk's hood—is apparently too drunk to drive: revving their engine then slamming on the brakes, before finally pulling out of the lot.

Ambrose's keys jingle and I glance over in time to see the lights flash on a black SUV. He opens the passenger door for me, and I peer in. The car is newer and so immaculately clean it has to be a rental, but no decals cling to the windows. There's nothing to give a sense of who he is or what I'm getting into. I note the electronic lock controls on both doors, but the locks themselves are the type that can be easily pried up should I need to flee. Good.

"I'm not trying to trick you." He holds out his hand, his car key resting on his palm. "Here."

I flinch, afraid to touch his skin again, but am I more afraid of feeling a connection or do I fear the hidden strength in him? The predator lurking just below his calm surface. My eyes dart from his hand to his face. Is it weird, him forcing me to take the key from his hand, or am I overthinking things? Does he feel it too, that jolt when we touch? Is that what he's after?

"Go on. Take it." His features are calm, but a muscle along his jaw clenches.

My fingers twitch toward him, but I freeze, balling my hand into a fist. "You could have a spare."

"Search me, if it pleases you." He turns a slow circle, smoothing the pockets of his jeans to demonstrate that they're empty. He doesn't even carry a wallet.

He faces me, extending his palm once more. I reach for the key, sure his hand will close on mine, but he just stands there. As soon I have the key clenched in my hand, I feel a little better. Safer. A little foolish for making a big deal out of nothing. My fist tightens around the key, and I climb in, settling my bag on my lap.

His head dips toward my bag. "I can put that in back, if you like."

I shake my head, clutching the bag tighter. He gives me a sad smile and closes the door. A moment later, he climbs into the driver's seat where he silently stares out the windshield, his hands folded in his lap. For the first time, I notice he's without a coat, despite the chill, and his lean arms are unmarked—rare in Portland. Everyone has tattoos these days. His only possession is a black cell phone—a newer one that makes mine look like a dinosaur—nestled, dark-screened, in one spotless cup holder.

I wait for him to speak as I watch a whiskered homeless man, wearing a black garbage bag over his head in place of a poncho, meander across the parking lot. The wheels of his shopping cart clatter over the uneven asphalt and catching in flooded potholes.

When he finally he speaks, his voice is so soft I have to hold my breath to hear. "We're called Hahmi. Myth and fiction call us vampires, though most of what you've heard is false. Daylight," he gestures to the windows, "doesn't harm us. We are not living dead or undead, and it takes more than a stake through the heart to kill us."

"Vampires?" I almost laugh. This has to be a joke. But his face is serious, and his eyes remain fixed on the long, pale hands cradled in his lap.

"Vampires, demons, devils—these mythoi are all in some part inspired by our kind. Thanks to many centuries of effort, only those thought to be infirm believe we exist at all, and nearly everything known about us is utterly fictitious—aside from the obvious: blood and teeth." His lips draw back, exposing animal-like fangs.

I shrink back against the door. How did I never notice his teeth before?

"Yours will change too, once you feed." His face relaxes, his killer's teeth once again hidden behind soft lips.

"You realize this sounds incredibly crazy, right?" Even as I say this, I remember the way my vision pulsed at the sight of Lisa's throat, that smell. It was her blood I smelled rushing beneath her skin.

The corner of his mouth twitches and smooths. "I know, and I'm sorry you had to experience the change like this, that we couldn't first talk about it. There wasn't time. It's better than the alternative, isn't it?"

I hug my bag in my lap. My memories from that night are patchy, but I remember blood—too much blood. There's no way I could have survived. Even with urgent medical treatment. For a second I see my mom strapped to a cot in the ICU, thick gauze bandages circling her wrists. It was no use. Too much blood lost. I blink back tears as a small crack appears in my carefully assembled wall. I will not cry. Not in front of him. I examine the charcoal upholstered roof until my tears agree not to ruin my life. "I know. I'm just freaked out, and I feel like death. My head—"

"You haven't eaten. I'm surprised you haven't shut down."

Our eyes connect for an instant, a flash of violet. Goose bumps break out on my arms, and I look away.

"The first time is the most important. It must be fresh, and always within the first few hours after consciousness has been regained. That was . . ." he prods the display on his phone and *tsks* softly, "nearly eight hours ago."

"Fresh . . ." I can't bring myself to say it. I keep thinking about sharp teeth and Lisa's neck and that smell. "Like from people? Killing people?"

"Killing isn't necessary, though there are times when you will want to." He gives me a knowing look. "I don't kill innocents. That said, learning when to stop can be difficult. Blood awakens something . . . primal in us."

I remember how Lisa struggled in my arms, and I'm ashamed at how much I enjoyed it, how it made me want her more. "What if I refuse?"

His shoulders sag slightly and a pained smile flickers across his lips. "Without blood you will grow weak. Eventually you'll slip into a coma until someone revives you."

"And if no one does . . . then what? I die?"

"I imagine your body would mummify and eventually turn to dust." His hand twitches toward me before returning to his lap. "Just try. That's all I ask."

I take a deep breath. It isn't as if I've never thought about killing someone. That horrible woman who always complains about the temperature of her latte, my perv of a boss—ex-boss. But those were harmless fantasies.

"You don't need to kill anyone. Just try a little and see how you feel."

"But, won't they turn into a vampire too?"

He raises his hand. "We're Hahmi, not vampires—"

I roll my eyes. "Whatever, same difference."

"It's more involved than that, changing someone, but we'll get to that later. Much later. First, let's see to you. Blood will help, I promise."

"You really believe this, don't you?"

He nods. "Completely."

The rain picks up again, drumming on the roof, frothing the murky puddles in the potholes. The homeless man huddles in his garbage bag, snugged up against the side of the bar, a dour look on his weathered face.

I swallow hard and pass Ambrose the key. "Show me what to do."

Chapter 7

Fifteen minutes later, we're back at the house I fled. Seeing it in the gathering dark does little to ease my fears. It looms like a haunted house in a horror film. All it lacks is a gate—one of those spiked, wrought iron ones. Ambrose circles around to a large garage, empty save for a vague car shape under a canvas dust cover in the far corner.

We enter the foyer where the massive marble and oak staircase stretches upward, he turns into the first door on the right, and flips on the lights. Row after row of bookshelves span from floor to ceiling. A tall track ladder in the opposite corner grants access to the higher shelves.

"Wow!"

He looks down at his hands like a shy child. "I am glad you like it. I spend much of my time here." He skirts a wide table and a tall claw-foot couch, making his way to the back corner. "You may leave your bag in here if you wish. No one will disturb it."

"Where are we going?"

"Downstairs."

I pause at the small couch, eyeing the book-lined walls, the tall, curtained bank of windows. There are no stairs. I'm about to say as much when he reaches the last bookshelf and nudges a square of molding along the bottom with the toe of his boot. With a series of clacks, the shelf swings aside, revealing a set of narrow, gloomy stairs. I try to hide my astonishment, but he notices and his eyes gleam with something like pride.

I know I should be wary, but the intrigue of a secret passage is too much to resist. I slide my bag beneath the couch, and we descend into the gloom.

At the foot of the stairs he stops, his keys jingle as he unlocks a door, and we pass into a low-ceilinged earthy-smelling basement lined with doors—all closed. Two along the back wall have what look like hinged tray slots cut into the metal about three feet above the cement floor. They remind me of prison doors. Does he keep people down here? Is this a trick?

I freeze at the foot of the stairs while Ambrose takes another set of keys from a peg at the entry and unlocks the farthest of the two cells, swinging the door wide.

He turns back to me. "Don't be frightened."

Yeah, don't be frightened, I only want to lock you behind a steel door. But if that was his intent, wouldn't he have locked me down here in the first place? Feeling mostly convinced, I take a few steps closer and peer in.

Bare brick walls and a cracked cement floor shift under the dim, unsteady glow cast by a single bulb. The bulb buzzes softly as if there's a fly trapped inside, flickers once, then steadies. At the back, a man lies on a low metal cot. He's too big for it by far, and his legs jut off the end.

He *does* keep people down here. I open my mouth to protest, then I notice the man's cropped blonde hair and the scratches across his cheeks and forehead. "I—I thought you killed them."

Ambrose's head tilts to one side. "I never said—Ah! Of course. That certainly explains why you ran." He laughs, shaking his head. "It seems in my effort to ease you into this I was too vague. I let the other two go. They were impressionable and on their way down a dark path, but they weren't violent by nature." He tips his chin at the man on the cot. "But this one has a darkness. I don't believe in a god or a cosmic judge, but so long as I have to feed on humans, I might as well sift the chaff. I thought it would be easier on you if he was your first. This way if you accidentally kill him, you won't feel too terribly bad."

There's really no way to know if he's lying about the others. But it doesn't matter, this clearly isn't his first time. I'm sure he's killed many—how many? I don't want to know. This is all too weird. But I certainly don't want to go near that crew cut jerk, let alone drink his blood or whatever it is I'm supposed to do. But I creep closer, careful to stay outside the cell, afraid to wake the sleeping man.

Despite my attempt to be silent, Crew Cut wakes and struggles to his feet. The scratches on his face are red and swollen. I hope they're infected. His eyes lock on Ambrose and he puffs out his broad chest; surely he thinks it makes him look tough. "Hey! You can't keep me locked in here! What the f—"

"Be quiet. Lie on the bunk and stay there." Ambrose's voice is firm but calm, like he's directing a disobedient child.

I almost laugh at the ridiculousness, like this jerk's going to listen, but Crew Cut's mouth snaps shut, and he returns to the cot without another word. The cell is silent, the only sound the intermittent buzz of the bare lightbulb overhead.

"What . . . what just happened?"

"We can control humans." He says it as if he's just stating a basic fact, no big thing. He beckons me. "Come. I will teach you."

My eyes shift from him to Crew Cut.

"It's okay. He won't hurt you. He can't move unless you or I tell him to."

"How do I know you're not just saying that?" Then the worst occurs to me. Maybe this is all a sick game. I shouldn't say it out loud, but I can't stop myself. "How do I know this isn't a trick? You two could be working together."

Ambrose gives a surprised laugh, and his lip curls. "You think I would associate with that?" He shakes his head. "Perhaps we played some vile sport together at university?"

I'm not sure what's more ridiculous: the image of Crew Cut, a broad-chested caveman, and Ambrose, a pasty English bookworm, as cohorts, or the thought of Ambrose playing football.

"You're safe, I promise. He can't disobey a command."

I clutch the steel doorjamb. "So if I tell him to chew off his arm, he will?"

"Yes." Ambrose's lips pinch together. "And if that's what it takes for you to believe, by all means do it. But it's not something I should like to see. He is despicable, but no one deserves so much as that."

I don't want to believe even though Ambrose's face is unwavering, but part of me wants to do it anyway. Crew Cut remains frozen in place, staring at the ceiling, oblivious. Would I see some change, a moment's hesitation, a reaction before his teeth clamped down on his own flesh? My fingers loosen on the door jamb and I enter the cell.

Ambrose shifts at my side. "Please, don't."

I can almost feel the tension in his words. "I'm not going to." I'm pretty sure I'm not lying. Pretty sure I was never seriously considering it. Pretty sure I don't even believe any of this is real. I turn to face Ambrose. "What should I do?"

His shoulders relax a bit, and mine do too—however slightly. "The first time is the hardest. The thought pathway has to be established. Once the path is created you'll be able to see into his mind with just a thought. Try asking a question—it will help you access his memories. You don't even need to speak out loud, just project your words into his mind. I often ask that they show me the worst thing they've done. If it's something unforgivable, they die. If not, I take only what I need, erase myself from their memory, and send them on their way."

"You can spy on people's minds? What about privacy?" Can he access my thoughts? It seemed like he could at Vox, but now I'm not so sure.

"It may not be right, but it's a useful tool. You'll see."

"That's creepy."

He shrugs and nods to the man on the cot. "Give it a go."

I take another step toward the cot and stop, looking back at Ambrose. "What if someone's really messed up and they don't think what they've done is wrong?"

"Impossible, even for extreme psychopaths who seemingly have no remorse. It may be a result of social conditioning, but part of them knows they've done wrong." He smiles, a brief flash of vicious teeth. "They always confess."

I repress a shudder. "Why do you kill them? Couldn't you just scare them into being better people?"

Ambrose's face darkens and it looks as if he's going to say something, but he shakes his head and points to the cot.

I turn back to Crew Cut and project Ambrose's question. I feel ridiculous. Am I doing this right? I'm sure I won't see anything and Ambrose will just say I did it wrong. At the same time, I'm afraid of what I *might* see. Afraid I'll see myself, naked and bloody.

Before I know it, images flash behind my eyes.

A wedge of light spills into a bedroom, pushing back the shadows, defining the edges of a child's bed. A chest at the foot holds a hoard of stuffed animals. A small girl lies sleeping, the blankets pulled up beneath her chin. Crew Cut sits on the edge of the bed, gazing down into the girl's face. He eases back the covers, and she stirs.

"Mommy?" The girl's voice is thick with sleep.

Crew Cut's face, a slightly younger version, drops close to hers. "Shh. Remember what'll happen if you're not quiet?"

The girl nods, her wide eyes glassy. "Don't let Mommy take me to the place for bad kids."

"Then be a good girl. Take off your PJs and close your eyes."

I don't want to see what comes next, but I can't make it stop. I'm trapped between two worlds—half in a dreary cell, half in a shadowy bedroom.

"You have to break free," Ambrose says, but his voice comes from far away.

I'm shaking. No, Ambrose is shaking me. I'm in a cell. No, I'm in a little girl's room. No! Arms close around me. I try to jerk away, and they tighten.

"It's okay. It's over now," Ambrose whispers, smoothing my hair.

I smell clove and honey, and the images fade. I sag against him. Finally, my breathing slows and he releases me.

"Which was it?" he asks. "The little girl?"

I nod. "There are more?"

"Many. She was his first. His own sister." He shakes his head. "It can be intense the first time, but it gets easier—you'll see." He steps to the cot and turns the man's head, exposing his neck. "His blood will help. Try a little."

Even from where I stand, I can see the blood beneath his skin, pumping and swirling. It makes me dizzy. I take a deep breath and kneel on the cold cement at Crew Cut's side. His neck is ringed with dried blood and grime, and the sour stench of sweat drifts up to greet me. I lick my fingers and rub his neck, wipe it clean with my sleeve. It's the best I can do without hosing him off out back. Nothing can be done about the smell.

"Try not to think about it." Ambrose says at my side. "Close your eyes and focus on the smells."

"I *am* smelling! He stinks!"

"That's just the surface. Go deeper. Close your eyes." His voice is calm, but slightly patronizing.

I sigh, shut my eyes, and try to ignore the tidal wave of stench. Ambrose is right—a moment later, another smell takes over, one that's warm and alluring despite the filth. I concentrate on that smell and lower my face to Crew Cut's neck, trying not to think about the sweat and grime as my lips instinctively seek the place where his blood's vibration is strongest.

My teeth graze his skin, and there's a flash of pain as my incisors grow and drive into his flesh. He gurgles softly deep in his throat, and my mouth floods with warmth. The flavor is beyond delicious and completely unexpected. His blood works through my body, and every cell tingles, expands, aches for more. This is what I need. I climb onto the cot and clutch him, drawing him closer. Something snaps under my grip. He sucks in a sharp breath and whimpers. Behind me, Ambrose says something, but I ignore him. Nothing matters. There is only the blood.

Hands are on my shoulders, pulling. I fight to stay with the warmth, but it slips from my grasp, and I'm jerked back into reality.

"I said slowly! You're going to kill him."

Everything is muted, the world is too dim. Everything but the man on the cot. He seems to glow, pulse. He's trembling, and I tremble too; my body hums with energy.

"I need more." I start toward the cot, but Ambrose holds me back.

"Wait. You don't need to kill, just wipe his memory and send him on his way."

I stare down at the man's face. His eyes are closed, peaceful, as if he's sleeping. I remember the weight of his foot on my chest, threatening to crush me like an insect. How they laughed as he and his friends surrounded me. I remember what he did to that little girl. "No. I want to kill him. I want him to see how it feels to be weak."

"Even so," Ambrose says, "you should practice controlling him. Make him forget the feeding. Just command him, and it will be done."

"Then I can kill him?"

"Then you may do with him as you please." One corner of Ambrose's mouth twitches. A smile or a frown?

I study Ambrose's face, and on impulse, I try to reach into his mind. But there is nothing, only blackness. He must be able to block it. "Why—" I mean to ask him why I can't see into his mind, but that would be admitting I tried.

Ambrose raises an eyebrow.

"Never mind." I wave a hand and return to the cot.

A jagged red oval marks Crew Cut's jugular. My teeth did that. It looks like he was mauled by a dog, but already the wound is clotting, only a thin trickle of blood seeps out. I shake my head and focus on my task. *Forget,* I project.

Crew Cut's eyes pop open. "Where am I? What's going on?" He licks his dry, cracked lips, his eyes shifting from me to Ambrose and back again.

"You're safe now," Ambrose says. The corner of his mouth twitches. "Isn't that right, Sasha?" He glances at me, his eyes encouraging me to play along.

I feel like the world's worst actor. "Yeah. The police should be here any minute." Ah, shit. I shouldn't have said police—a guy like him might not be so thrilled about the idea of cops. But the man on the cot just nods, wincing a little, clutching his shoulder.

He groans and, with some effort, sits up. "My shoulder's messed up. Feels like something's broken."

Ambrose smiles down at him reassuringly. "Help will be here soon. While we wait, what's your name?"

"I'm . . ." The man's face goes blank and his mouth falls open. "I can't remember—"

"Silence," Ambrose says in a harsh whisper, cutting him off. Ambrose's eyes meet mine, and his tone softens. "See, you have wiped too much. Memory is a fickle thing; tampering with it poses the risk of permanent loss. Which is why you should be specific about what one should forget. Right now he doesn't even know who he is, let alone what he has done."

I frown. "I want him to remember me. What he did." Unwanted images seep into my mind, and my breath catches.

The man on the cot is saying something. Ambrose pinches the air, and the sound cuts off as if he's turned an invisible volume knob. Something about it is familiar though, and for an instant my vision goes violet and a chill runs down my spine. "What—"

Ambrose waves his hand dismissively "Focus on the matter at hand." He tips his head toward the cot. "It might not be too late since those memories are recent."

I turn back to Crew Cut, and as I project that he remember me, his eyes widen with recognition.

"You—"

"No. You don't get to speak. People like you are what's wrong with this world, and you all seem to find me."

He must see something in my face, a homicidal glint, because he leaps to his feet and lunges at me, but it's like he's running underwater. I jump aside, easily avoiding him, and he crashes into the wall.

"You can control him," Ambrose whispers.

Crew Cut turns and charges me again.

"Don't move!" I shout.

He freezes mid stride, wobbles, and crashes to the floor face first. He doesn't even attempt to brace his fall. I look at Ambrose, who nods approval.

"Roll over," I command. Crew Cut flips onto his back I struggle to repress a smile. As weird as all this is, my power over him is intoxicating. I can do anything I want, make him do anything I want. I sit on his chest and stare into his murky eyes. There's no remorse in there, only a narcissistic sense of entitlement. But still, I'm surprised to find I feel no pity for him. I truly want him dead. Blood trickles from a cut on his forehead and trails into his hair. I can smell it, and my mouth waters. My new teeth find his neck, and his life slips down my throat like velvet fire.

❈ ❈ ❈

Ambrose kneels across from me. "He's dead." He lifts Crew Cut's arm and lets it flop back to the cement. He sounds a little shocked, like he didn't think I had it in me.

I surprise myself with a laugh. The sound is startling in the small cell. I feel good, whole for the first time since ever. Most importantly, my headache is completely gone. "I thought it would be hard to kill him," I say. "I thought I might feel bad. But I don't."

"Do you believe me now?"

I drop my eyes to the body between us. "I guess I have to. I just drank this guy."

"You have a bit—" His hand twitches toward me, then pulls back. He points to the corner of his own mouth instead. "—just there."

I wipe the side of my mouth, but he shakes his head. "Other side. A little higher—here, let me . . ."

He reaches out again, and this time I lean forward, awkwardly angling my chin up at him. His thumb brushes the corner of my mouth and his fingers graze my neck, sending a hot shock through my body. He shifts closer, and for an instant, I catch his scent. I forget everything, the corpse beneath me, the strangeness of the last few hours, caution. I can see, can think about, only one thing: his lips. I lean closer.

"I'm sorry." He quickly pulls away and turns his back on me. "Forgive me, that was wholly inappropriate."

I take a deep breath, trying to quell my conflicting emotions, to deny the growing desire threatening to take me over. Ridiculous—I don't even know this guy. "It's okay. I mean, I don't want to rush into anything—" *Oh, god. Please shut up.* "—not that we're—I mean, not that I don't want to—Ugh!" I cover my face with my hands, mashing my palms against my lips to force myself to stop talking.

His hand settles on my shoulder, then slips away. "It's hard for me too. It's been a long time since I've had someone to care about."

I lower my hands and look up at him. "You don't even know me."

"Not yet, but I hope to. I want to."

I watch his face, looking for tics, trying to figure him out. I want to ask why he cares so much, but I can't bring myself to say the words. My eyes drop to the dead man. "What about him?"

Ambrose looks down, eyes widening slightly as if he's seeing the body for the first time. "Ah, yes. It's important that we cover all evidence of a kill. Our existence must remain hidden."

"Why? It's not like we can get picked up by the cops. You can just mind control them, right?"

"It is not the humans we hide from. True, we don't want them to know we exist, but they're not a threat. We hide because we are hunted."

"Like vampire hunters?"

He laughs. "Far worse, I'm afraid. It's the Quaadah."

"The what?" It sounds more like he choked on a mouthful of rocks than uttered an actual word.

He closes his eyes for a moment as if gathering his strength. "This is going to sound strange." His eyes snap open and bore into mine. "I said I'd explain once you were fed. We, Hahmi, humans—all life on Earth, for all we know—were created by an alien race called the Quaadah."

And now I've heard it all. "That's—wait . . . you're serious? Aliens? Like little green space beings?"

His eyebrows scrunch together, and he paces the cell like an anxious zoo animal. "Yes and no . . ."

Oh, god. He *is* serious. I struggle to keep a straight face. "Have you been watching *Ancient Aliens*?"

"Pardon?" He halts mid stride and gapes at me as if I'm the one speaking gibberish.

"I mean, sure even Stephen Hawking says aliens exist and that they probably want to kill everyone, but creating life on Earth? I don't believe that X-Files stuff." This is where he's supposed to confess it's all a joke and we'll have a good laugh. I won't even be mad. Well, maybe a little.

He shrugs, shaking his head. "Yesterday you didn't believe in vampires."

I open my mouth to respond and sink back on my heels. I've got nothing. He's right. What's one more? Hell, maybe unicorns and fairies are real too.

He kneels beside me and draws a deep breath. "You don't have to believe me, but if it's proof you require, you may get it soon enough. It's getting worse."

I don't want to feel the chill his words produce, but I'm powerless not to. Whether it's true or not, it's no joke to him. "What's getting worse?"

"People have been disappearing."

"By people, do you mean humans or whatever you—*we*—are?"

"Until now, they've never taken humans, but something's changed. It has become so bad the media has picked up on it; though, it's far worse than they know. Hundreds are taken every day."

I remember the news story, all those missing people. Was that really only a few days ago? I glance down at Crew Cut. "Why? What do they want?"

He forces a smile. It looks more like a wince.

"What? You don't know?"

"Anyone who could say for certain is long gone."

"But why would they create us only to kill us?"

"They didn't technically create *us*, not as we are; but they created Hahmi long ago, millennia before you or I existed. Those Hahmi weren't like us. Similar, yes, but you and I were once human; the original Hahmi never were. They're hybrids, closer to the Quaadah than to humans. Popular consensus says they were created to keep the human population in check. The Quaadah knew that without a predator, humanity would overrun the planet."

"Is that why they're hunting us, to regulate our population?"

"Maybe, but I think it's a bit more complicated than that." Ambrose is on his feet again, pacing the small cell. "We call ourselves Hahmi after the beings who made us, but our existence is accidental. The Hahmi population was never intended to grow. The original Hahmi were engineered to be sterile. The trouble began when the originals discovered they could infect humans—they created us without the Quaadah's knowledge, if you believe the stories. So maybe the Hahmi were originally created to control humanity, but they are long gone. We're all that remains; we're a constant reminder of the Hahmi's defiance."

He stops pacing, looks down at me. "Perhaps the Quaadah don't care at all, and it's just that they prefer to regulate humanity on their own. Maybe it's sport, or maybe they want to end us all and reclaim Earth for themselves. We can talk theory all day, but it's all speculation." His voice is calm, but his hands shake just slightly; he stuffs them into the pockets of his jeans and shrugs like it's no big deal.

A seed of unease roots in my gut, and I wonder how much he's hiding from me, how much of his calm exterior is an act. "Where are they now?"

"Who? The original Hahmi? Extinct. We're all that's left."

"No. The aliens."

"No one knows. If we could find them, we could fight, but—"

"Then, what *do* we do?"

He pushes his hair from his face. His hands are steady now; how much effort does that take? "What we've always done. Keep quiet and cover our tracks. Starting with bodies." He tips his head to the dead man beside me. "Burning is the preferred method."

"Burning? Where? How?"

"This place used to be a full service funeral home. The crematorium is still functional." He steps from the cell and looks back. "Come, bring the body."

I gape at him. "Bring him how? Have you seen this guy? He's more than twice my size."

His mouth does that quick little twitch. "You'll manage." His eyes fix on something behind me, and this time he does frown. "I'll have to have someone take care of that mess too."

I follow his gaze over my shoulder and spy the bloody mattress. "Sorry."

He shrugs. "Occupational hazard. Come now, that body's not going to lift itself." He turns away, but not before I see a mischievous grin spread across his face.

I roll my eyes at his back. Real fucking funny, jerk. The dead man at my feet is impossibly huge. I grab his wrists and yank hard, and he shoots up, nearly toppling me over backward. I squeeze him in an awkward bear hug. Just when I think I have a handle on him, his knees buckle and he sags in my arms. A low, tuneless groan escapes his bluing lips, and I jump away as he crumples to the floor, skull thudding against the concrete. "He's not dead!"

Ambrose laughs over his shoulder. "Perfectly normal; it's just trapped air escaping."

"You knew that would happen!"

Ambrose turns. He's grinning widely, and I can see how he must have looked as a child. It takes all I have not to grin back. I'm supposed to be mad, dammit! "Let's call it payback for calling me—how did you put it? Batshit?"

"Technically that was a compliment," I mutter, shaking my head.

❈ ❈ ❈

Ambrose flips a switch, and the room fills with fluorescent light, revealing horrid 1970s avocado-green tiles. There's a stench of charred bone with just a hint of formaldehyde. It reminds me of the fetal pigs in biology, their tiny grey-pink snouts smashed against vacuum-sealed plastic.

A heavy metallic door dominates the back wall. It looks like a giant version of the walk-in refrigerator at the restaurant where I worked in high school. And that's exactly what it is, only this one holds bodies instead of produce.

Ambrose tugs the door latch, and cold, death-scented air billows out. "Set him there." He points to a vacant gurney in the back.

The cooler's not that deep, but it seems like there are several miles between here and there. There are so many bodies, some covered with white sheets—stiff feet peeking out, paper tags clinging to big toes like bland ornaments—and others are tucked into anonymous black zipper-bags. Others lie exposed. "Are these all . . . yours?"

"Not all of them. Some come from local hospitals, nursing homes, and the like. A tech comes in to burn them three times a week. It's all aboveboard." His face scrunches slightly, in a way that makes me think of Lisa. "Mostly, anyway. The rest is, you know." He taps his temple. "Mind-control." He nudges me forward, his palm at the small of my back, and I step into the cold.

I know all these people are dead, but my pulse thrums in my ears. At any moment, I expect a cold ashen hand to shoot out and grab me. It's like that time mom took me trick-or-treating at a nursing home. I was six, and that old woman had looked dead too, until her clammy, grey fingers clamped on my wrist. Her eyes had a far-away sheen, a slack half-smile hung on her cracked lips. I realized with blind panic that she wasn't going to let go.

I shiver and adjust Crew Cut's dead weight on my shoulder. I make it to the empty gurney and struggle to position his uncooperative noodle-limbs. I may be stronger now, but no amount of strength will help me with this body. What I need is an extra hand, but Ambrose is no help; he watches, leaning against the heavy door, his eyes twinkling with suppressed laughter.

After several minutes, Ambrose's face sobers. Perhaps he's tired of watching me struggle? "That's fine, leave him. He's fine just like that. Come. I want to show you something."

Chapter 8

In the gloom of the shadowy mudroom, I make out a second door across from the one leading out to the garage. An iron umbrella stand full of swords, of all things, sits beside it. "What are those for?"

"Practice. But that's not what I want to show you. Come." He pulls the door open and waves me through.

Gravel crunches beneath our feet, and moonlight pours in through a high glass ceiling, filtering through vines and branches, casting everything in a soft silver glow. The delicate smell of flowers fills the air, all familiar, yet different. I can almost see the individual scents like colors.

"Overwhelming, isn't it?" He closes his eyes, breathing in.

"It's beautiful." I step off the pebble path onto a patch of grass and sit under the canopy of a sprawling magnolia tree. A strand of hair flutters against my cheek in the mild breeze. I brush it away and turn to find the source. High up on the opposite glass wall, a fan churns the air, its slight mechanical hum barely audible over the trickle of a nearby fountain and the soft ribbit of frogs. If I didn't know better, I would swear it's June instead of late February.

I run my palm over the soft grass and watch Ambrose sniff the cup of a low-hanging magnolia blossom.

"How do you maintain all this?"

He releases the flower and sits beside me, folding his long legs before him. "We have a few employees—"

"We?"

"It's just us for the moment, but five others reside here. I'll introduce you to everyone."

Nervous knots bunch in my stomach. I've never been good at meeting new people. I say the wrong thing or nothing at all, coming off as either an idiot or stuck up. Maybe both? I make a mental note to clear out well before introductions start.

He smiles reassuringly. "They're good people. Most of them I've known for centuries, all except Giric. He came to us from another house in Greece nearly a decade ago. He can be a trifle dramatic, quick to temper, and a touch annoying at times." Ambrose glances over his shoulder toward the house. "He follows me about, so I have to keep switching up my hiding places. Luckily, I never see him out here. I don't think he knows we have an atrium." He shrugs. "I shouldn't divulge this before you've had a chance to meet. It's unfair of me to color your first impression. I'm sure he means well, he's just lonely."

I blink most of his words are lost on me, all I can focus on is one, but that can't be right. "Did you say *centuries*?"

He nods. "I was given Cnila Hom in the autumn of 1663."

"But you would be—"

"Well over three hundred." He looks back at me flatly, daring me to challenge him.

Over Three hundred? The words echo in my head, and I want to reject them. I want to scream at him, call him a liar. But I know he's telling the truth. Can I argue logic after all I've seen? I draw a deep breath. "So, we don't age?"

He shakes his head. "Not in that sense. With blood, our bodies regenerate—indefinitely, I presume, but no one can say for certain. Cleis, the one who turned me, has been alive for a thousand years, possibly longer, but physically, we remain the same as when we were reborn." He chuckles lightly, shrugging one shoulder. "I suppose that's another thing the stories got right. Some of them, anyway."

I can't even fathom the concept of living that long, let alone forever—or at least until the sun expands and roasts everything. The thought of living to see the end of the Earth is chilling. The misanthrope in me always hoped for disaster—apocalypse, plague, the ruin of the world constructed by people—but I never believed I'd live long enough to see it. Of course, on the surface I think I'd love it, that I'd thrive in the chaos, but then I remember men like father and the ones from the club, and I know I'd neither thrive nor survive. I'm a slave to this modern world; it's the only thing keeping me safe, and even that's not enough—but now . . .

I glance up to catch him staring at me. There's an intense look on his face, and I can tell he wants to ask something probing, possibly sappy, definitely uncomfortable. I better distract him, quick. "What's your story then? How did you— oh . . ." What he said earlier hits me, and my heart drops. Of course he's unavailable. "The one who turned you, Cleis? You're together?"

"Together?" His head tips to one side, then straightens. "No. Not in the way I believe you're suggesting. Cleis and I are merely friends. He and his spouse, Anne, live here. You'll meet them both soon."

"Oh." I watch my fingers twirl in the grass and shrug as if it doesn't matter, but my heart is beating so fast I can barely talk. *Just be normal.* "It must suck for Anne, being the only woman in a house full of guys."

"I'm not sure she minds, but it wasn't always quite so imbalanced. There was another woman, Ecrin. She's gone now, but the two of them never got on well."

"Were you close?" I regret asking. It comes across as desperate, like I'm trying too hard to puzzle out his history.

"I like you, Sasha, as a friend and more, if you're willing." He reaches across the grass and his fingertips brush the back of my hand, gently, briefly, leaving a trail of warmth that spreads through me.

My cheeks are on fire. I should have known he'd see through that. Is it really so hard to be direct instead of playing games every time? What's that they say about insanity? Insanity is doing the same thing over and over and expecting different results. Guilty.

He's staring at me again. *Say something, anything else.* "Where is she now?" I can't even remember the name of the woman we're talking about. I keep my eyes on the grass otherwise I'll look at his lips and—*he said he likes me.* I realize he's still talking and yank myself from my thoughts.

"—but Ecrin's been missing close to twenty years now."

Missing? Goose bumps break out on my arms and my eyes snap to his—his lips suddenly the furthest thing from my mind. "The Quaadah?"

"Most likely." Ambrose shrugs casually, but tension lurks along his jaw.

Or maybe I'm imagining it. Either way, he clearly doesn't wish to elaborate. I want to push him but I sense he won't budge. "So, did Cleis find you bleeding in the street too?" It's not the question I want to ask. Close, but I can't bring myself to ask why he changed me. He probably wouldn't answer honestly anyway, and sometimes it's better to not know

"No, nothing like that. I don't believe he had a particular reason. He just wanted company, or maybe it was fate—if you believe in that sort of thing." He plucks a snowy magnolia petal from the grass and rolls it between two fingers. "Would you care to hear my story?"

I nod and scoot a little closer, glad to be relieved from speaking, for a moment, at least.

He takes a deep breath. "My family ran a modest inn about five leagues south of London—not more than a few beds and a stable. Late one night, in walks this wild-haired traveler. His hair is calmer these days—Anne's to thank for that—but back then he was all flyaway flaxen curls." Ambrose's face glows with fond memories. "I asked where he'd traveled from, and he responded with a grin and something vague and existential like, *everywhere and nowhere*. I assumed by his worn, dusty clothes and unruly hair he was one of those roving men, most likely insane, and I resigned myself to hearing no news of the outside world. We'd get that sort now and again. So long as they paid and didn't make trouble, they could stay. He paid for a drink—overpaid really, giving me a sixpence when only a penny was due—but he never touched it. Instead he drank from a leather flask, as if he was afraid of poisoning. It was blood of course, in the flask, so I later learned.

"Then he said, 'You want to see the world?' I was sure he was talking to himself. His back was turned and he hadn't moved except to tuck his flask back into the pocket of his coat. It was only the two of us in the room, you see. But his words gave me such a jolt. It was as if he'd plucked the thoughts from my mind. Because it was true—I had always dreamt of traveling. But we hadn't the means, and there were duties, obligations. My mother passed when I was young, so it was just my father and me and my two younger brothers. That was life. It was hard, but we got by better than some.

"At last Cleis faced me and said, 'Yes, you.' He might have even added *boy*, though he was hardly more than a sprog himself—at least in human years. He said he sought an apprentice of sorts, and that I would do. It was odd the way he said it, as if I'd already agreed. Before I could say a word, he reached into the satchel at his feet, pulled out a leather purse, and tossed it onto the bar. It thudded with an important, heavy jingle. 'Consider that your first payment. That should more than cover your absence.'

"I pulled the purse strings, and inside saw a gleam of gold, at least twenty sovereigns. I could hardly believe they were genuine. It was, at the time, the most money I'd ever held. He told me he was taking passage on a ship early the next morning, and if I was coming, I should be ready by dawn.

"That night I hardly slept. I worried if I closed my eyes I would wake and it would all have been a dream. I rehearsed what I would say to my father. I would tell him straight away, and before he could utter a solitary word, I'd plunk the purse into his hands and flee, leaving him to contemplate the contents in stunned silence.

"My worry was for naught. Morning came and Cleis was there, waiting. He spoke to my father, who was surprisingly understanding. I'm sure Cleis helped in that regard, sometimes I wonder what he told him. I've never asked." Ambrose waves his hand, "But anyhow, I made my hurried goodbyes, then Cleis and I rushed to the docks."

Ambrose pauses. "I didn't learn about the flask—about what he was, what I would become—until we were well at sea. Then I was given the real choice."

He falls silent, and I shift in the grass at his side. "What if you'd said no?" I ask. "He had you on that ship—it's not like you could go anywhere."

Ambrose's brow furrows slightly, and he is quiet for a moment. "I don't know. I suppose he would have sent me back home, but he knew I would accept. A chance to see the world, live forever, learn. How could I pass that up?" He studies me intently. "Would you have said no?"

I shrug and look away. I imagine, the only drawback to living forever is watching your loved ones die, but I don't have that problem. Lisa is the extent of my close relationships, and even what we have is superficial. Not that it matters anymore; It's not like she'll ever talk to me again.

"I'm sorry." His voice is soft, fragile; his eyes drop to the crushed petal in his hand.

I shake my head but don't elaborate. I probably wouldn't have said no, but I can't admit that. It would reveal too much, and the conversation would shift into uncomfortable territory: He'd want to know why I would have accepted. My plans for the future . . . my feelings for him. The question I want to ask is *why me?* Maybe that's how he gets his kicks. He's one of those guys with a savior complex. He wants me to feel indebted to him—I owe him my life, after all. It's a form of control; a debt like that can never be repaid.

I give him a plastic smile. "Then what happened?"

His eyes find mine, and for a moment I see a spark of determination like he'll pursue his question, but then it's gone. "Then, I followed Cleis around the globe until I could stand it no longer. A few of us settled here."

"That's it? You just traveled? What did he need an apprentice for? Just someone to carry his luggage?"

Ambrose laughs and stretches his legs out in front of him. "If only. No, he was forming a militia. He trained us to fight the Quaadah, which we did, but not well. We were mostly successful in getting ourselves killed. It's a miracle any of us survived at all."

"You've fought the Quaadah?"

He nods. "We did a lot of wandering about, searching. The Quaadah are difficult to find when you're looking for them, but they seem to sense the moment you let your guard down."

I scan the dark glass surrounding us. Are they out there right now, watching?

He follows my gaze. "You're safe here."

I watch the windows a moment longer, waiting to catch movement out there in the dark. At last I tear my eyes away. "What are they like?"

"At a glance, they're not much different from us or humans, only they're bald and sexless with unpigmented skin. Largely you can identify them by their eyes: entirely violet, no sclera."

I suppress a shudder. Of course they'd be violet—like his . . . like mine.

His hand brushes my shoulder, and I jump. "You're safe here."

"It's not that, I—" My mouth snaps shut. I can't tell him how that color makes me feel. He'll think I'm nuts.

He looks at me, eyebrows drawn, like he wants to say something.

"I'm fine, really." I shift and his hand falls from my shoulder. "Where's Cleis now?"

"Looking for the Quaadah. Hahmi generally fall into one of two categories. Many are like Cleis, militant, actively seeking an end to the Quaadah and their hold over us. They follow a half-understood path set out by the Order thousands of years ago. Then there are some like me, who think all this fighting is pointless. We've been at it for centuries and it's never done a bit of good. We just want to lead normal lives—or as normal as our circumstances permit."

"What's the Order?"

"I've been asking the same question for centuries. It was started by the original Hahmi, what was left of them anyway. These days they're all gone—extinct. Everything we know about the Order is little more than rumors from eras past. It's like that children's' game, Telephone: the story's come out all muddled. From what I understand, the Order is like religion, those who follow it guard it and uphold the ideas, but no one stops to question why."

"What kind of rumors?"

"The only thing they seem to agree on is that Hahmi were created for a higher purpose, then our creators—the Quaadah, left Earth with the promise that they would one day return to lead us to this unspecified higher purpose, when we were ready. Instead, the Quaadah returned, and what was supposed to be a celebration turned into a slaughter. Hahmi have been hunted ever since."

"So much for a higher purpose."

"Exactly, and so, the Order believes the Quaadah here today are imposters, they're not really our creators. Their word for them—" He shakes his head. "I can't recall their word, Cleis could tell you, but translated it means half or partial soul. It's all nonsense, a story created to give themselves hope. As is the habit of thinking beings frightened of self-reflection. We desperately need to feel that we're not alone, not forgotten, that our lives mean something other than what is apparent. I once thought people obsessed over religion because they're afraid of dying, but I know now they're just afraid to live."

"What does that even mean: half soul? The Quaadah don't have a full soul? Why, because they're immoral for killing people?"

"I don't know what they mean by it, and I doubt anyone alive today truly knows." His gaze shifts to the branches overhead. "Not all killing is immoral."

I give him a sideways look. I read somewhere that all killers have a story they tell themselves; what they do isn't wrong, they're helping, or their hand was forced by some god, or they have to keep the basement wall soaked with blood to keep the horrible creatures on the other side from breaking through. Psychos. "How many people have you killed?"

His eyes drop to mine. "That's not the point." His smile is tight, like he's holding back. "The people I kill deserve it. They violated others. Their actions are inexcusable."

And that's Ambrose's story. His gaze is intense, challenging me to disagree, but can I, really? It's not like the legal system; there's no innocent until decided guilty. It's certain. One glimpse into a person's mind and all is exposed. Am I just buying into his story? Do I have any other choice? I shut my eyes and hold them closed. I almost expect to snap awake in my apartment to find this was all a really weird dream.

His hand brushes my shoulder, shattering my escapist fantasy. "It wasn't my intent to overwhelm you. Enough of this dreary talk; it's far too lovely an evening. Tell me about yourself."

I shrug and pluck a blade of grass. "What do you want to know?"

He leans closer and I smell cloves and sun-warmed honey. "Everything. Tell me something interesting."

I shrug. "Nothing exciting here. I was born, grew up, worked menial jobs—" I gasp, and my eyes fly to his.

"What? What is it?"

"Oh god! It's Tuesday!" I leap to my feet and pat my pockets, searching for my phone, then I remember it's in my bag in the library. "Shit! I completely forgot about this interview."

"Ah, yes. Eggs and legs."

"How—you were listening? At Vox?"

Ambrose laughs loudly, startling a bird resting on a branch above us, and he doesn't stop. Between gales he makes an owlish hooing sound as he tries and fails at speaking. Tears squeeze from his eyes, and he presses his hands over his face.

I try to be annoyed, but I can't help smiling even though I have no clue what could be so funny. "Thank you. I'll be here all week."

He laughs harder, rocking back and forth in the grass, and all I can do is watch and shake my head.

At last, the rocking stops, and he gulps a mouthful of air. "I'm sorry." He wipes the corners of his eyes. "All right." He nods, draws a deep breath, and he's back. Calm and composed. "That was terribly embarrassing. My apologies, again."

"What's so funny?"

"It's nothing. Forget it. Please, sit." He tugs my hand trying to get me to return to the grass.

I pull away. "No. Not until you say why you're laughing at me."

"Come now, I wasn't laughing at you. It's just, the past few days have been intense—" He waves a hand dismissively. "Why would you want a job—especially one so awful as that?"

"Hey, beggars can't be choosers. Do you know how hard it is for me to find a job? I'm not exactly a people person."

He takes my hand again and this time I reluctantly drop to his side. "None of us *work*—not in the capitalist sense anyway. There's no need." He wipes his eyes again, shaking his head. "I suppose you could if you wanted."

I shrug. I technically have enough savings to cover next two month's rent, and it's not like I'll be spending money on groceries any time soon. I also would have no qualms about brain melting my vapid landlady into believing I've paid up for the year. The place is overpriced anyway. "Then how do you—"

"Stocks, mostly. It's all incredibly dull. Alan has people who know people. It all works out. Barring that, you can demand nicely. Not the most ethical solution, but certainly a means to an end. But that's a worry for another day. You were telling me about you."

Actually, I wasn't. I squirm under his gaze and pull at the grass. "There's nothing to tell. Compared to all this, my life's boring, or it was."

"I don't believe that. You are anything but boring."

I roll my eyes and look away, hoping he'll move on before I begin to blush. I desperately hope he's not one of those people who feels the need to comment on the fact that I'm blushing. Yes, my face *is* red. Thanks for noticing.

"Well then, what of your family?"

No, I'll not be discussing family; this isn't a pity party. "What happened after you left home? You mentioned your dad and brothers. Are they around?"

He gets that look again, and for a second I'm afraid he'll push harder, but his determined smile fades, replaced by a weary sadness.

Way to go. Of course a story about his family can't have a happy ending; he's older than god. "I'm sorry. You don't have to answer that." At least I haven't lost my knack for saying the wrong thing. I make a mental note to add it to the list of skills on my résumé. I need sensitivity training.

"No, I don't mind. When I left with Cleis, I promised I'd only be a year . . ." His shoulders sag as if under a heavy weight.

"But?"

"But time got away from me. I returned too late. The plague took them."

The plague? Like *the* fucking plague? The fact of his age finally sinks in; this guy is ancient. It's funny to think how I once worried about my ex being eight years older—and in the end, it still wasn't enough; men mature much more slowly. Maybe several centuries was what it took. I realize I'm staring, open mouthed, and I remind myself to make the appropriate empathy sounds. "Wow. I'm sorry." Super comforting. About that sensitivity training . . .

A thin smile stretches his lips. "It was all long ago."

"Would you have turned them?"

He's silent for a long brooding moment. When he finally speaks it's hardly more than a whisper. "I don't think my father would have accepted, but my brothers, maybe eventually, once . . ." His voice catches, and he drops his eyes to the grass. ". . . once they were grown."

I want to reach for his hand, to comfort him, but I can't move, I can't find the right words, and then I'm rambling. "My parents are dead too. My dad died four years ago. A car accident. He was wasted—no pun intended. But seriously, he was drunk, as usual. He crashed into a concrete center divider. My mom killed herself when I was fifteen, a few months after I left home." Just like that, messy fragments of my life come spilling out. I haven't talked about my family in years, but here I am, telling this beautiful stranger my secrets. Exchanging sob stories.

"I'm sorry." His hand finds mine in the grass.

I shrug. "My dad was no great tragedy. He did the world a favor. It's just too bad it didn't happen sooner. My life, and my mom's, might have been different."

He squeezes my hand. "Why did you leave home?"

"It's a long and not so pretty story." I've already said too much. Could he make me forget my past? I want to ask but I'm afraid. Who would I be without my memories? What if something goes wrong? Would I lose myself completely?

He stares at me, his eyebrows cinched together. I wonder what he's seeing. Is he's spying on my thoughts right now? How much does he know? I drop my eyes to the grass. I'm all too aware of his hand on mine. I worry that if I move he'll pull away, and at the same time, I wish he would.

He sighs, a sad sound, releases my hand, and settles back on the grass, crossing his arms beneath his head. The bottom of his shirt pulls up, exposing a sliver of porcelain flesh. I force my eyes away, but not before he catches me looking.

"Lie with me," he says. "Look, the clouds have cleared and the stars are out."

I know I shouldn't, but I stretch out next to him, our shoulders touching. The stars burn overhead. They look so much brighter than I remember, and I imagine I feel their heat across the distance, tiny flecks of warmth on my face.

He shifts at my side, props himself on an elbow, and I can feel his gaze on me.

"What?"

He smiles softly. "I wish I knew what you were thinking."

"Why? Can't you read my mind? The whole time at Vox I had this suspicion."

He looks down at the grass between us with a guilty smile. "No, only humans."

I bolt to sitting. "I knew it! You spied on my thoughts!" I hide my face in my hands, peeking out from between my fingers.

He bites his lip. "It was a shameful thing, but I couldn't resist."

"That's *so* not fair. I thought a lot of . . . You suck!" My cheeks burn, and I shake my head in my hands.

The grass rustles as he shifts closer. "I was a perfect gentleman. Others might have taken advantage of such thoughts."

"Oh, you're so noble." My voice comes out muffled against my palms.

He brushes my shoulder, and I look up. "Are you saying you wouldn't have peeked had the situation been reversed?"

I glare at him, knowing I would have, and that I tried, but I'm not about to admit that. I hope my face isn't as red as it feels.

"I meant to tell you earlier, but you were so upset. And . . . I do share your feelings. If you'd heard my thoughts, you wouldn't think me a proper gentleman at all. Please, I beg your forgiveness."

He gives me such a look of remorse; I can't stay mad. I roll my eyes and sigh. "Okay, fine. I forgive you, but on one condition."

He straightens and scoots even closer, his shins less than an inch from my knees. "Certainly, anything. I am yours to command."

I laugh at his child-like eagerness. "Tell me the most embarrassing thought you've had in my presence."

It's his turn to blush, and I take great pleasure in watching him squirm as he decides whether or not he'll play along.

"Hey," I say, "you have the better end of this deal. You already know how I feel about you."

"Do I have to say something from Friday night or should it be more recent?"

"Quit stalling or I'll increase your penance."

He smiles, and it's sweet and innocent, and I'm glad for my private thoughts.

"When you caught me watching you dance . . . I may have had an impure thought or two."

"Go on. You're not getting off the hook that easy."

He sighs and flushes brighter. "I wanted to feel your lips on mine. I wanted to know the scent of your skin. I wanted to know how your blood would taste." He smiles awkwardly. "I wondered if the carpet matched the drapes—is this shameful enough? Need I go on?"

I fall back in the grass, laughing. "No! No, you can stop. Your debt is paid, sir."

He lets out his breath, but his cheeks still glow. On impulse, I grab his hand and draw him close. His hair tickles against my cheek and his lips find mine, soft and warm.

"Thank you," he says, sitting back.

I look at him, puzzled. "For what?"

"For keeping me honest. For making life more interesting. For listening to me. For coming back."

I shrug. "You saved my life, remember?" I lean toward him, ignoring the warning voice in the back of my mind. I'm tired of being cautious. Can't I have a little fun?

He pulls away, his face earnest. "Will you stay with me?"

"What? You mean stay the night?"

"Yes." He smiles shyly. "And the next, and the next."

"I . . . I don't know." He can't be serious. Why is he asking this now? We hardly know each other, and he wants me to move in? Though with all his mind spying, he probably knows me better than I know myself. I tug his shoulder, trying to pull him back down in the grass with me, to shut him up, change the subject, but he won't budge.

"It's just—" he begins.

"Shh." I hook a hand around his neck, my fingers working into his hair, drawing him closer. His lips meet mine, warm and sure.

"What on Earth is going on out here?"

Ambrose and I jerk apart. A man with flawless olive skin stomps down the path toward us, clenched fists peeking out from gaudy white lace. His chestnut hair falls in perfect tousled curls around an insolent cherub face.

I instantly dislike him.

"I'm entertaining a guest," Ambrose says, a hint of irritation in his voice.

"Since when do you have *guests*?" The man peers at me over Ambrose's shoulder, his face sour. "I haven't seen you before. Which house are you with?"

Ambrose sighs and helps me to my feet. "She's not from a house, Giric, she's new. This is Sasha."

I smile and offer my hand. He glowers at me, his lip curled as if I'm some unclean thing not worthy of breathing his air. I want to find a rock to hide under, or maybe use it to bash in his pretty little face.

Giric's gaze flashes back to Ambrose. "New? By whose authority?"

"I don't need permission to turn someone."

"If you attended meetings like the rest of us, you would know those laws were reinstated in the sixties." He turns his attention back to me. "You're under arrest until you can be tried."

I can hardly believe this guy is allowed to be in charge of anything. He's completely unstable. I want to ask what he's talking about, but the shock on Ambrose's face suggests I should keep my mouth shut.

Ambrose glares at him. "She won't be going anywhere with you."

Giric leaps forward, nearly faster than I can see, and in an instant, he has me in his grasp with my arm wrenched up behind my back.

"Let her go. Now." Ambrose's voice is cold and sharp.

Giric tugs my arm higher. A breathless scream escapes my lips as the tendons in my shoulder strain. I struggle against him.

"Be still or I'll rip it off," Giric whispers against my hair.

The muscles in my shoulders burn, but I force myself to freeze. The tension eases.

Ambrose tenses and it looks as if he's about to charge. "I said—"

"Stop there!" Giric shifts, and cold steel presses against my throat.

My flesh wants to crawl away from the blade, but I hold still, afraid to breathe.

"Back off Ambrose or I'll send her to Purgatory." Giric twists my arm higher.

I know he wants me to scream. I clench my jaw, but I can't help but whimper as the metal bites into my skin. I imagine his satisfied smile.

Ambrose winces, sucking in a breath, then his eyes harden and he takes a step forward. "Have you lost your mind?"

"Step back and I'll do everything I can to minimize your penalty. Otherwise, I'll add obstruction to your charges, and you can join her in the cells."

The blade slips, and I gasp. A warm trickle slides down my neck into my shirt. My eyes lock on Ambrose, but he's focused on Giric. I want to beg him to get me out of this.

Ambrose shakes his head. "It is you who will be needing help once Alan hears of this."

Giric huffs against my hair. "If that's how you want it. You're both under arrest."

He wrenches my arm higher. My eyes water and my breath rushes out. It takes everything I have not to struggle, and still the blade sinks in. It stings, searing into my skin.

"Go on Ambrose, lead the way to the cells." He tightens his grip on the sword at my throat. "Or I swear, I'll do it."

I will Ambrose to cooperate, begging with my eyes, before this psycho ends up cutting my head off. It feels like the metal is already halfway embedded in my neck. Would I survive decapitation? Logic says no. Saliva pools in my mouth but I don't dare swallow. I'm afraid even that small movement will force the blade deeper.

Ambrose's eyes soften and he nods slightly, mouth bowed, shoulders slumped. "I'm so sorry," he says to me.

❊ ❊ ❊

I follow Ambrose down the stairs, all too aware of the knife at the base of my neck. The basement seems darker than before, more isolated. Its damp musty smell seeps into my lungs, and I can almost taste it.

"Unlock the first cell and take a seat on the cot," Giric instructs Ambrose. "Leave the keys in the door."

Ambrose opens the first of two steel doors with the low tray openings and steps inside. His cell is exactly like the one that held Crew Cut, except that the dim bulb suspended from the ceiling is steady and quiet.

Giric nudges me forward with the blade. "Lock him in and open the next one."

My hands shake as I reach for the keys. Ambrose gives me a half smile and a gentle nod, then he's sealed behind heavy steel. Surely he meant that smile as a comfort, but it looked more like the gesture of one resigned to his fate.

"Go on, next one's yours," Giric prods me between the shoulders with the tip of his blade.

I step into the second cell and bite back panic as the door slams shut behind me and the lock turns. The light flickers, buzzing, somehow angrier than before. That'll get old fast. It could almost be a new form of torture. I turn to the cot; the filthy mattress is still there, blood soaked and yellowed with dried sweat. I flip it over, but the opposite side is just as nasty. Is that piss? Charming.

I return to the door, crouch, and push the tray flap. It opens outward, providing a small window into the main room, and I mash my face against the narrow rectangle. I can't see Giric, but I know he's there because his muffled voice floats in through the narrow gap. He has to be at Ambrose's door. I hold my breath, straining to make out his words, but it's no use.

Then his voice swells, and he adopts a saccharine, cheery tone. I imagine the sneer on his cherub face. "You shouldn't be so rude. No one knows you're down here; I could *forget* to report you."

Giric pops into view, coming toward my door, picking through the keys. Before he can fit the key in my lock, there's a soft chime. He jumps slightly, like he's been caught doing something wrong. The chime sounds again, and he removes a phone from his pocket; his lip curls as he glares at the screen. A second later, his eyes snap back to my door, and I flinch as he catches me watching. He gives me a shark's smile that makes my skin crawl. I want to back away, let the flap fall closed, but I'm frozen.

He crouches at the slot, inches from me, and waves his phone. "I have to take this," he whispers, "but I'll be back. Don't go anywhere." He sneers and shoots to his feet, bringing the phone to his ear. "Giric speaking." His voice is chipper as he stalks to the stairs. A moment later, the lights in the main room wink out, and the only light left is that which leaks out from the dim, stuttering bulb behind me. I hear a soft rumble, and I imagine it's the bookcase sliding back into place to conceal the stairs.

"Ambrose?" I whisper through the slot. I hold my breath, listening for a response, but there is only the tireless buzzing. I call a little louder; still nothing. I stand and inspect the door. Maybe I can pick the lock? Yeah, with what? I quickly realize it doesn't matter anyway: a metal plate has been welded over the lock. I kick the door, a mistake. The door is solid steel; it hardly even makes a noise. Waves of pain consume my foot and I blink back tears. There's no getting out of this room unless someone comes to release me, and the only one who knows we're down here is a mental case on a power trip.

How long until Giric returns? He can't leave us down here forever, right? I glance at the useless cot across the room. Maybe I could make a weapon out of the frame? There's nothing better to do. I lean the disgusting mattress against the wall, flip the frame on its side, and bounce on one of the legs. It bows slightly, and I slam my boot down until the metal crimps. After a few minutes, the leg snaps free. The end is jagged and sharp. It probably won't kill him, but if I could stab him in the eye . . .

I sit in front of the door, holding the tray flap open, the bar across my lap. The main room remains dark and silent. I wait. Hours seem to pass, or maybe days. The buzzing is hypnotic and my eyelids grow heavy. I jump up before I can fall asleep, stretching, jogging in place until I'm not tired anymore, then I return to my vigil.

I call out to Ambrose again, but there's still no answer. What is he doing?

My arm grows tired of holding the slot open, and inspiration strikes. I remove my shirt from beneath my hoodie and wedge it in. It takes up a third of my view, but leaves both hands free.

A million years later, my bones throb from sitting. I try pacing, my steps sync with the buzz, and I find myself walking in time. I count sixty-second increments, stooping down to scratch a hash mark into the crumbling cement after every ten. The buzz, my footfalls become a mantra, and time loses meaning. Numbers stop being words, and I forget what comes after forty. Half of the cracked floor is filled with hash marks, some run into cracks, and I realize I don't remember where I made my last mark. I give up and drop in front of the door to continue staring into the dark.

❈ ❈ ❈

I snap awake and my head knocks against cold metal. I can't see. My hands fly to my face and my fingers poke into my open eyes. I'm blind!

My heart races and my throat threatens to close. He's going to kill me, and I'll never see him coming. I flail in the dark, and there's a clatter as something metallic falls to the concrete. I try to stand, but my legs are heavy and dead and I pitch over.

A moment later I understand. I fell asleep cross-legged, cutting off the circulation. As if brought back by the thought, the blood rushes back in. My sudden blindness is forgotten as painful cold-hot prickles flow from my groin to my toes and back again. I writhe on the floor, breathing hard, struggling not to move my legs but helpless not to. At last the pain subsides.

Phantom lights swim in the dark, neon green and pink. Someone breathes, loud in the void, and I realize it's me. I hold my breath and perfect silence expands around me, as if I'm in the vacuum of space. Is space silent? Something is missing.

The buzzing.

I'm not blind, the light burnt out. How long have I been in here? How long will he keep me here? I remember the headache and dizziness from earlier. How long can I go without blood, how long before I mummify or whatever?

There's a soft metallic squeak, then a rectangle of light glows in front of me, spilling in through the open slot in my door. I peer into the main room. A stream of light slants across the floor from the direction of Ambrose's door.

"Sasha?" Ambrose's voice fills the darkness. He's nearly screaming, and his voice is hoarse, frantic.

"Yeah?" I yell back. My heart is pounding so hard I can hardly breathe. Something is wrong.

He says something, but his voice is muffled.

"What?" I shout through the gap. "What happened?"

His voice swells in the dark. "You weren't responding. I've been calling for hours."

"I fell asleep."

"What? Sasha?"

"I fell asleep." It feels weird to be screaming. "My light burnt out and my mattress is filthy."

"I'm sorry. I can't—"

"What?" I strain to hear. Did he say more? I want to scream in frustration. There's so much I want to ask, but not like this. I huddle against the door focusing on the stream of light. I picture him crouched at his own, his long limbs folded up like he's some exotic insect, listening, waiting for me to speak.

There's a rumbling overhead and Ambrose's flap squeaks closed, taking the light with it. Someone is coming. My throat clenches and I paw at the floor, searching for my makeshift weapon. Feet thump on the stairs. The sound is deafening in the dark, though I know it can't actually be that loud, and still my hands come up empty. Keys jingle, and my heart leaps into my throat.

My hand brushes cold metal, I squeeze the bar so hard my knuckles crack, and flatten myself against the wall beside the door just as the light flicks on in the main room, flooding into my cell through the open slot. I adjust my grip and try to gauge where Giric's face will be. He's only a few inches taller than I am. *Giric.* It's like the sound a cat makes before hacking up a hairball.

My legs vibrate with nervous energy, ready to run. I consider my bag under the couch in the library and shake my head. There's no time, I'll have to leave without it. The key turns in my lock and the door swings open. A silhouette appears in the doorway. I launch. He's taller than I remember, and I correct my aim.

He moves so fast, knocking the bar from my hand, and throwing me to the ground. The back of my head thuds against the cement, and lights explode behind my eyes. I thrash below him but I'm easily subdued.

"Shh. Be still. No one will harm you."

It's not Giric. The voice is deeper, richer, and very English. Each word is soft and deliberate. The face hovering over mine is drawn and stern, but his eyes are kind. He's handsome in a scholarly way, his hair a soft copper-brown with a touch of grey at the temples.

The flap in Ambrose's door creaks open. "Hello, Alan. I see you've met Sasha."

Alan eyes me warily. "If I let you up, are you going to behave?"

I nod, smiling awkwardly, feeling like a jerk. I take his offered hand and allow him to help me to my feet. "Sorry, I thought you were the other one."

Alan raises an eyebrow and releases Ambrose from his cell. "It seems we have much to discuss." He sweeps an arm toward the stairs. "Shall we?"

I yank my shirt from my cell door and follow them up, delighted that I'll be able to leave with my bag after all.

❧ ❧ ❧

In the library, grey daylight streams in through the high windows, but which day? How long were we down there? It couldn't have been that long. Though my stomach is convinced it's been weeks. Alan directs Ambrose and me to the couch, and I notice my bag is still underneath. I glance to the door, and the foyer beyond. I should just leave. *Thanks for your help, but wow, look at the time! Gotta go.* But am I ready to feed on my own? Should I just drop off my bodies? Do I sign up for pick-ups? Jesus, I've only killed once, am I really so heartless? But I don't have to kill, right? I can stop and erase myself from their memory. I think I can stop. It's not like I have to worry about getting arrested. But then I remember what Ambrose said. He's not afraid of humans, it's the whatever he called them.

Ambrose takes a seat, leaving a space for me. The couch looks impossibly small; I'd have no choice but to sit touching him. Well, maybe I could stay for just a moment. Just to be polite, and so we can figure out this feeding business. Why do I bother lying to myself?

I sit beside Ambrose, and as his thigh touches mine, I'm comforted. My desire to flee, evaporates. I feel like I can handle anything so long as he's touching me.

Alan drags a chair over from the table and settles in front of us. He turns to Ambrose, his face serious. "I'm at a loss as to where to begin."

I catch movement outside the door, and a curly-haired blonde guy knocks loudly on the doorframe before stepping into the library. "Have you seen Anne? I'm afraid I've set her off again—Oh . . ." His eyes shift between Alan and Ambrose, then to me as if he's just realized he's interrupting something.

Annoyance flickers across Alan's features, then it's gone. "Cleis, this is Ambrose's friend, Sasha." Alan waves a hand toward me.

Cleis laughs. "Ambrose Durling doesn't have friends."

Alan gives Cleis a warning glance.

"It's only a joke." Cleis looks Ambrose over, his eyes seem to pause at the intersection of my and Ambrose's thigh. I resist the urge to pull away. "Appears to be a mite more than friendship." Cleis's face lights up "And you're new! Ambrose, I didn't think you had it in you, after all that talk of responsibility. The two of you look great together, honestly, all the black; very serious, but fantastic."

"Oh, we're not—I mean . . ." My cheeks burn. I attempt to scoot away from Ambrose, but there's nowhere to move. I glance at Ambrose. He looks as embarrassed as I feel. "We just met." Yes, just met, kissed once—er, several times. Oh, and disposed of a body together. Yeah, we're practically married.

Cleis smirks playfully, oblivious to or unconcerned with the discomfort he's causing. "Please. Anyone with eyes can see there's something between you two."

"Cleis, I thought you weren't back until tomorrow?" Ambrose says, clearly in an effort to change the subject.

"We returned early, but we're heading right back out, the car's coming at four. I just hoped to see Anne before I leave again."

Alan clears his throat, and glances pointedly at his watch. "It's ten past four."

Cleis sobers. "Right, I better be off. Ambrose, we have much to discuss when I get back. Hug Anne for me when she turns up. Tell her I won't be long, then I promise we'll take that trip to Canada that she's been going on about."

Ambrose nods and just like that, Cleis sweeps from the room, his chaotic energy trailing in his wake.

Alan tents his fingers on his knees and leans back in his chair, eyebrows drawn in concentration. A moment later, he sits up. "The crematorium technician called me complaining that he heard shouts through the walls. You know how I feel about holding people in the cells. It's such a hassle having to clear his memory every time."

Ambrose nods innocently. Now would probably not be a good time to mention Crew Cut.

"So, I pop down to investigate his latest complaint, expecting some half-dead sap, but instead I find the two of you. Perhaps you'd care to enlighten me?"

Ambrose shifts next to me, his thigh brushes mine. "I assume you have not talked with Giric?"

"Not since last night." Alan cocks his head, narrowing his eyes. "Why?"

Ambrose relays most of the story, beginning with finding me dying in Jamison Square—omitting my freak-out and that we killed Crew Cut downstairs. He ends with Giric locking us up and threatening to leave us there.

Alan's thick eyebrows draw together, forming a deep worry line. "He certainly failed to mention this when I spoke to him. Giric has indeed handled this poorly, but he is correct in part, except that nonsense about a trial—I suspect that was just him being dramatic, as is his way. It hasn't always been the case, but now, turning another is a process. I've been lenient with you, Ambrose. You stopped attending the meetings decades ago. I know how uncomfortable they are for you, and until now, it's never been an issue. You feed responsibly and keep to yourself." Alan adjusts his shirt cuffs. "Of course, there are exceptions in the event of an emergency, as this clearly was. But don't you see, you got lucky. This could have gone badly. What if she reacted erratically? She could have run off. Imagine the damage—remember the fiasco with Ada?"

I clench my fists and hope my face doesn't give me away. Just how much trouble would we be in if Alan knew the full truth?

Ambrose sucks in a sharp breath. "What happened with Ada wasn't—"

"I know, I know. It's not the same. My point is, these aren't arbitrary rules; they keep us safe, and we all must obey them. As for Giric, I can't imagine what got into him, but with his threat to hold you in the cells, and the fact that he didn't tell me about this when we spoke last night, I'm left with no choice but to relieve him of his duties. Such behavior shall not be tolerated."

Alan stands, smoothing the creases from his slacks, and he faces me. "I am deeply sorry for all you've been through. It's no way to begin a new life, but I'm glad to welcome you. Anyone who gets Ambrose out living life is all right by me." He laughs and returns his chair to the table. "As far as I'm concerned, Sasha, you're welcome in this home. Anne will surely appreciate having another woman about. There hasn't been another woman around since—" Alan's face becomes pinched and he shakes his head. "Well, it's been a long time, and I'm sure Anne tires of being surrounded by us beasts. For the time being, you'll have to share a room with Ambrose. We haven't a spare." He dips his head toward Ambrose and stage whispers, "He's a pretty decent chap."

"Oh, I have my own apartment, but thanks." What is it with these people? Is it an old fashioned thing? Oh god. Do they expect Ambrose and I to get married?

Alan's smile shrivels and his eyes snap to Ambrose. "I see you've not told her."

Ambrose winces.

"Told me what?" My stomach clenches. Just what I need, another surprise.

They exchange a glance. Ambrose gives a what-can-you-do shrug, and his eyes squeeze closed.

Alan fidgets with his sleeves then clasps his hands before him. "New Hahmi must live within a house for at least the first two years—"

"Two years? But—" My brain screams *run*. Run now. Would they really stop me? Lock me in that cell forever? Ambrose's head is in his hands, his fingers clenched in his hair. It's almost as if he's the one being put under lockdown. It's a nice act, but I don't buy it for a second. It's what he wanted all along, isn't it? He asked me to stay with him in the atrium. As if I'd have a choice. Would he really have given me a choice at any of this? If I had said no to becoming a blood-drinking freak, would he have let me die?

Alan raises his hands, palms out and cautious like someone dropped in a lion pit. He draws a deep breath. "Please. It's just a precaution."

It's all too much; I leap from the couch. "You can't do this!" Ambrose touches my shoulder, and I whirl on him. "You lied to me! You said I could leave."

"I'm sorry. I didn't want to frighten you. I just thought once you—"

"I know this comes as a shock." Alan takes a step toward us, face drawn, his thick eyebrows mashed together. "But do see this is for the common good. You are not a prisoner; you are kin, but there are rules. I promise you're safe here."

Safe. Everyone keeps saying that, then I end up in a cell or they tell me we have to hide from the evil aliens, or is that a lie too? Something to keep me scared, keep me here? I can't help the betrayal I feel. It's always the same, every time I try to trust someone. Am I cursed? I look between these two men, both with identical looks of sad concern. As if they care. There's no way I'm getting out of this. Especially if I continue to make a scene, but they can't watch me every second of the day. I take a slow, deep breath and force myself to calm down. "Sounds like I don't have a choice."

Some of the tension eases out of Alan's shoulders, but his eyebrows are still bunched. "I am sorry. Usually there is more time to integrate. Please don't put blame on Ambrose—it's beyond his control. If you must be angry with someone, let it be me." Alan turns to Ambrose. "There's a gathering at Prisca's tomorrow night, a little welcome home for the troops. I expect to see the both of you there." He shakes back his cuff, and glances at his watch. "I hate to leave you two thus, but I must deal with Giric."

Alan breezes from the room, and I stare after him, desperate to look anywhere but at Ambrose. Neither of us speaks and the silence is suffocating until his boots shuffle on tile, and before I can stop myself, I've turned to face him. Our eyes meet.

"I wanted to tell you in the atrium. I would have if Giric hadn't—" He drags a hand over his face and drops back onto the couch with a defeated sigh. "I've let you down. I can see it in your face." He stares at his hands clenched in his lap, his shoulders slumped. "I wish we could start over." He's quiet for a moment, then his head jerks up and his shining eyes hold mine. "Tell me honestly: Would you have come back if I said you wouldn't be allowed to leave? Would you trust me more if I stopped you from running; If I locked you up? I could have, you know. I heard you leave."

I swallow hard. I don't want to hear his excuses. He's right, but that doesn't make this any less wrong. Any less weird.

He gives a little huff of a laugh, shaking his head. "I didn't think so, and I don't blame you. You don't know me. All I can say is I have your best interest at heart. Please . . ."

114

I stare into his wide, imploring eyes. It's obvious he suffers, and a part of me is glad. He should suffer. But I find myself nodding. "Fine. I'll stay." What choice do I have?

His eyes close, and he lets out his breath. "Thank you. I won't let you down again."

I smile weakly. How many times have I heard that line?

Chapter 9

mbrose parks and we step out onto a dark, litter-strewn sidewalk. I've never been to this part of town, and it doesn't look like anywhere I should be. He said we were going out for dinner. I'm still adjusting to the fact that dinner is people. Sirens wail in the distance. Three hard-looking men lean against the chain-link and razor wire fence that surrounds an auto shop, smoking and drinking cheap booze from paper bags. Their raucous laughter competes with the loud music pouring from a strip club at the end of the street. I slip closer to Ambrose.

"There's nothing to fear." Ambrose's hand brushes my shoulder and falls away.

He's right, and I know I'm stronger now—I'm not a fragile human anymore—but this looks like the set of a thriller movie; the scene right before the cops find a dismembered corpse in the dumpster.

The men against the fence glance our way, speak to each other in hushed voices, then they're laughing again. Ambrose draws me in with an arm around my shoulders. I tense, before relaxing against him. How can his body feel so right against mine? Don't *even* think about that.

"They won't harm you. Look into their minds and see for yourself." He's not trying to be sexy, but his breath puffs in my ear and I shiver. I hope he assumes I'm shivering out of fear.

I'm submerged in their thoughts before I even realize what's happening. It's easier this time. Too easy, and I find Ambrose is right. These men aren't a threat to anyone but the gene pool.

I tear myself from their thoughts and turn to Ambrose. "Where are we going?"

He grimaces. The muscles along his jaw bunched with tension. "You asked about rehabilitation."

"What do you mean?"

"You'll see. Come, it's not far."

From the look on his face, this can't be good, but before I can ask any questions, he starts off in the direction of the strip club. I take a deep breath and hurry after him. The music swells as we near the club, and for a moment, I'm sure we're going in, but he passes the entrance and cuts through the parking lot.

Behind us, the club's door bangs open, and I turn to see a crowd of men spill out in a cloud of laughter. I catch fragments of their depraved conversation; they're arguing about which of them some stripper named Lucy liked best. *She only liked your money*, I want to scream at them, but I don't. I glance back at Ambrose, he hasn't slowed, and I trot to his side.

We continue across the parking lot, then turn down one side street after another, passing strangers without a second glance. Headlights bloom as a car approaches, and a man shouts something unintelligible at us as he speeds past. Ambrose leads me down another street and stops in front of a large corner lot. At first I can't even see the house past all the birdbaths, lawn gnomes, and cutesy Christmas decorations. It's like a bizarre yard sale where the owners, in a moment of clarity, realized everything they had was shit, and ran off in despair. I bet their neighbors hate them.

We start across the yard, picking our way through the labyrinth of grandma décor. I expect Ambrose to head for the front door, though I can't imagine who could possibly live here or why we'd be visiting. He said something about rehabilitation. Is this is the result of meddling—try to cure someone and they develop poor taste and hoarder tendencies? Maybe a quick death truly is a better option. He heads for the back, but he doesn't knock. Instead, he pulls out his keys and opens the door.

"What—"

He holds up a hand for silence and stands there, half in the doorway, head titled, eyes closed. After a moment, his eyes open, he presses a finger to his lips, then waves for me to follow. I step in after him onto a landing between two sets of stairs, and he locks the door behind us. The stairs to the right head up to darkness, but to the left, a yellow glow seeps from beneath a door at the foot.

He pauses to listen once more, then chooses left, and I follow him down. He unlocks this door too, and freezes, hand on the knob. He takes a deep breath like he's gathering his strength. Something about his caution sends a chill down my spine. It's completely irrational, there's nothing to fear. This is obviously a place he's familiar with, he has keys and everything, but I'm shivering all over. Suddenly I'm sure I don't want to see what's on the other side. I put my hand over his on the knob, and shake my head. His face is mostly shadows in the low light, and I can't quite make out the look in his eyes. His hand turns beneath mine, and he opens the door.

I'm not sure what I expected, but it's just an ordinary unfinished basement. Someone started adding walls at one point, but they didn't get far. There's one section of wall, but only half of the framed out portion has sheet rock, the rest is just a skeleton. As I step through the door, the smell, like an overripe outhouse, hits me. The sewer's probably backed up. How can anyone live like this? I want to ask Ambrose who lives here, but I assume it's still not okay to talk.

Ambrose motions for me to shut the door, then leads the way to the other side of the basement, skirting a rusty water heater and an ancient, mismatched washer and dryer with heaps of laundry scattered about, and he steps through the skeletal wall.

The smell intensifies with each step, and as I cross through to the other side, I find the source. It's not the sewer; the stench is coming from a large plastic dog kennel. Seeing it, Ambrose sucks a breath through his teeth and holds up a hand for me to wait. As he approaches the kennel, it shifts and a muffled but distinctly human whimper comes from inside. Then I see the twin mattress in the corner covered with dark stains that might be blood. The tension I've felt since we arrived intensifies, and without meaning to, my mind connects with the person in the cage.

Suddenly, I'm looking out through the crosshatched kennel door. A man peers in, naked save for his tan work boots, his body a hulking mass of wiry hair and sallow-pink flesh. A long red stick with a U-shaped head protrudes from his meaty fist. My stomach drops. *Is that a cattle prod?*

He works the latch on the cage. "Come on out now or I'll zap you right in the pussy." He presses the button on the handle and blue spark arcs between the contacts.

Crack of the charge makes my heart race, and the woman in the cage struggles to find cover against the back of the cage, her screams almost sound like words, but they are so muffled I assume she must be gagged, but I can't be sure. I can only see that she's naked and covered in dried blood and filth, forced to wallow in her own excrement.

The man's eyes gleam and the blob of flesh between his immense, hairy thighs twitches and he thrusts the prod into the cage.

I recoil from the images and stagger back. My eyes open, and I become aware of someone talking. It's Ambrose, he has the cage door open, and he's offering the woman a rumpled, but clean-looking, towel. "You're safe now. Come out."

There's no way she's going to come out, not after all she's been through, but she does. Then I realize, he must have compelled her. The first thing I notice when she crawls out is the tape around her mouth, encircling her head. I wince, seeing that it's been wrapped around her hair. That's going to hurt. Then I notice her hands. At first I think they're missing, but then I realize they've been taped into fists—it's so she can't work the cage latch. I don't know how I know this, but the intuition feels right. How horrifying would it be to know all that stands between you and freedom was a few layers of tape. It's enough to drive someone crazy. I want to puke.

Ambrose is still holding out the towel, then realizing she has no hands, asks if he can help secure it. Once the towel is around her, he pulls a small knife from his pocket, and after gaining her permission again—a solitary head nod—carefully frees her hands. She groans with relief, then in anguish, clenching and unclenching her fists. How long had she been bound like that?

Ambrose looks up to the tape across her face and winces. "I'll work as quickly as I can. You won't feel pain."

She nods, her eyes, wide and panicked, go blank as his suggestion sets in, and Ambrose cuts through the tape along both sides of her jaw, then slowly peels the tape away.

The tape has just cleared her lips when there's a sound from the stairs. The woman twists from Ambrose's grasp and dives back into her cage just as the basement door opens. It's the man I saw in her memory: massive and barrel-chested. Half his face is consumed by a patchy beard, and a sweat-stained trucker hat perches askew on his peanut-shaped head. He's wearing those tan work boots.

His eyes widen as he sees me, but when Ambrose steps to my side, the man bolts.

"Don't let him escape!" Ambrose shouts.

For a second I can't make sense of Ambrose's words. Does he want me to chase after this guy by myself? I want to ask, but Ambrose is squatting in front of the cage talking to the woman inside. With every second, the creep is getting farther away. His boots pound the stairs as he makes for the door. I'm helpless to stop him. Then I remember my lesson. It still seems impossible, but I reach for his mind, guarding against the memories I know I'll find within him, and I command to turn around and come back downstairs.

I know he can't disobey, but it's still shocking when he reappears in the doorway, his jowled face is deep red with anger or exertion, maybe both. I tell him to stay and he opens his mouth to speak, but Ambrose cuts him off with a terse command for silence.

"We can—" Ambrose winces and returns to the cage. He stoops to address the dirty woman inside. "Tell me your name."

"Amanda." Her voice is scratchy from disuse, hardly more than a whisper from the back of the crate.

"Thank you, Amanda. Sleep now, you won't hear Sasha and I talking until I say otherwise." He stands, not waiting to ensure his orders will be obeyed. He shrugs one shoulder and turns to face me. "No sense frightening her further. Earlier, I told you we can control humans. I've been experimenting with behavior in hopes of making them better people, but it's becoming clear that it only sticks if the deviant behavior isn't a manifestation of their true self. Some people act out of passion, fear, peer-pressure. Then there are people like him." He tips his head to the statue in the doorway. "The first time, he reverted after only three weeks. This time, it's been nearly two years . . . He was doing so well. I was so sure. Just last week—" Ambrose falls silent and his eyes drift up to trace the ceiling joists.

Guilt hits me hard, and it takes all my focus to not look at the cage, the bloody mattress, to not search for the cattle prod that has to be around here somewhere. "It's my fault isn't it? If you wouldn't have been busy with me, you could have stopped this."

It's like Ambrose doesn't hear me. He glances down at the kennel, shaking his head. "He was doing so well. I had hoped this time I'd done it. But I was wrong, and she had to suffer for it."

The implications of his words are frightening. In any other situation the idea of behavior modification and finding the essence of one's true self would be fascinating, but now, with this broken woman as a result, this insane house, I can't help but see it as something evil, a deep violation of consent. But who's consent? Hers surely, but isn't he a victim too? I stare at the man standing silent and frozen in the doorway. I don't like most people, but I always thought there was at least something good about everyone. Maybe not, but is that cause enough to justify experiments like this? "How long have you been doing this?" I try to keep my voice neutral; I'm not interested in an argument.

"Long enough. Too long." His eyes, watery and red-rimmed hold mine then slip away. "I'm going to help her now. Are you with me?" Ambrose's eyes catch mine again, daring me to push the subject. I don't and he turns back to the cage.

"Amanda, wake up. You can hear normally again." His gaze shifts to the monster by the door. "Where are her clothes?"

The man points, and I peer around the wall to see a black garbage bag next to a concrete laundry sink.

Ambrose crosses the room in three strides, takes hold of the man's arm, and looks back to me. "I'm going to take him to the car. We'll deal with him later. Would you mind helping her dress? I'll bring the car and park out front, then we'll get her to the hospital."

With a nod to Ambrose, I fetch the bag and kneel before the cage. "You're safe now. You can come out." I move aside to give her some space, and fish blue jeans, a white sweater, a pair of Converse, and a wallet from the bag. There's no bra or underwear to speak of; maybe she never had any, maybe the creeper has them squirreled away? It doesn't matter. I'm about to hand over her jeans when I remember she's covered in shit, and the towel Ambrose gave her only a moment ago is no better. My eye falls on the heap of laundry. "Hold on a second." I grab a towel from the pile of laundry, wet it at the sink, and rush back.

When I return, she's crawled to the front of the cage, and she looks up at me with wide hazel eyes. I smile—going for friendly, but she cringes and scuttles to the back again. I glance over my shoulder to see what freaked her out, but there's nothing. We're alone in the basement. Then I remember my fangs.

I kneel in front of the cage; she's shaking, pressed against the plastic, wide-eyed. I remind myself to use commanding language. "You can trust me. You're safe. Come out."

Her eyes go blank, just for a second, then she crawls out, clutching her filthy towel to her chest.

She's slender, dark haired, nearly the same age as I am, maybe a little older. A chill creeps up my spine. It could just as easily be me in her place. I shake the chill off. "Wash yourself with this, if you want, then get dressed. I'll give you some privacy."

She accepts the damp cloth, and as I cross to the other side of the room, I hear her softly whisper, "Thank you."

I nod before I remember she can't see me. "Ambrose is the one to thank." My response seems crass, and I rush to make amends. "I mean, sure—you're welcome." She is silent on the other side of the wall, but faintly there's the soft rasp of the towel on her skin, the rustle of clothing as she dresses. After a moment, the rustling stops. I wait. Will she tell me when she's finished? Should I ask? I give her another minute. "Are you decent?"

Her only response is a muffled sob. I peer around the wall. She's fully dressed now, but she's seated on the cold cement, her forehead pressed against her knees, arms wrapped around her shins as she rocks. Her crying gets louder as I step to her side, and my chest grows tight with anxiety. Should I comfort her or distract her? Will that make things worse? Is it rude to just compel her to stop crying? I'm still grappling with my options when Ambrose returns.

"The car's out front. Is she ready?"

Amanda's head jerks up. Her eyes are red but her face is mostly clean.

"We're going to get you some help. Can you walk out to the car with us?" Ambrose's voice is soft, disarming. He's good at this compassion thing. It seems so natural for him, unlike me; I just over analyze everything.

She nods, wiping her eyes with the heels of her hands. "What about—"

Ambrose stops just past the framed out wall. "It's over. He won't harm you anymore."

I offer her my hand, and after a second of hesitation, she takes it, allowing me to help her up.

We make it out to the car, and we're getting her comfortable in the backseat, when I realize the man is missing.

"Where—" I start, but Ambrose catches my eye and tips his head to the back where there's a massive black trunk. That's a good place for him.

❀ ❀ ❀

The ride to the hospital is silent. Ambrose pulls into the round-about in front of the double doors, and turns to face Amanda. "If you could forget all of this, would you want to?"

I watch Amanda's face in the rearview, her brow furrows as she contemplates the question. Would my face have looked like that if I had the chance to choose? Would I have wanted to forget? I like to think I would, but at the same time, who would I be without my memories? What makes me who I am? Is it how I've suffered? Is it all of my experiences? Can we be free from our memories, or are they with us forever like a long forgotten wound turned scar?

Amanda's eyes clear, and she nods, wiping at the fresh tears spilling down her cheeks.

Ambrose draws a deep breath, his eyes on hers. "The moment you step from the car, you won't remember this ordeal, either of us," Ambrose gestures to me and himself, "or how you arrived here. You will go to the front desk, check-in, and tell them you blacked out and woke up in an unfamiliar place. Get a rape kit, and have them check for internal injuries and STIs."

She opens the door, and I don't even need to read her thoughts to know the idea of putting all this behind her, of forgetting all of it, is strong in her mind, but Ambrose stops her as she's swinging her leg out.

"Before you go." Ambrose leans over me, takes a slim chrome case from the glove compartment, and passes her a business card with *Southeast Cremation Services* and a PO box address on the front in raised black letters. "Forward your bill to this address, and we'll take care of it."

"But won't that create a paper trail?" I know it's a stupid question as soon as the words are out of my mouth. "The memory thing, right?"

Ambrose only nods. Amanda tucks the card into her pocket and climbs from the car. The door bangs closed, and though it was she who closed it, she jumps at the sound. She peers in at me and Ambrose, her eyes clouded with confusion. Her thoughts reveal that she thinks she's just tried to get in someone else's car. She winces, mouths an apology, then steps through the double doors, her mind subconsciously constructing the story she would tell. She doesn't look back, to her, we don't exist.

❀ ❀ ❀

My second kill was easier. Maybe it was knowing what I am, or was it just that I didn't give him a chance to fight? I also never looked into his memories or thoughts. I didn't have to; I had already seen enough. I drained him in the walk-in fridge, him seated on a metal gurney, while Ambrose watched from the door. I guess that was a little creepy—Ambrose just watching—maybe not?

Now, up in Ambrose's room, alone, I wonder what Amanda is doing. Was she home by now, living her life, or still at the hospital? Ambrose said she wouldn't remember anything, but how perfect is his memory trick? Would she remember in her dreams? It's way too late to be thinking these kinds of thoughts, especially if I expect to have any hope of sleeping without nightmares. The blood refreshed me but my mind is tired, and it's not just the situation with her, but all of it: Giric, the aliens who want to kill us—as ridiculous as that sounds. It's just too much. Part of me wants to sleep simply to avoid thinking about any of it.

There's a curt knock at the door, then Ambrose slips in. "Sorry to keep you waiting. I had to fill out paperwork for the technician."

He really hadn't been more than ten minutes. I shrug and turn to the bed, stifling a yawn. "Which side do you want?"

He shakes his head and busies his hands with a scrap of paper pulled from his pocket. "The bed is yours. I'll sleep on the sofa in the library."

The thought of him folded up on that tiny couch makes my back ache. "You can't sleep down there." I should be relieved that he doesn't want to sleep together, and I am, but at the same time, I'm not. I tell myself it's the idea of getting into bed with him, having him so close, that freaks me out. One thing will inevitably lead to another, but that's only part of it. Mostly, I'm scared of being alone.

"It's more comfortable than it appears. I've been down there the last few days while you were recuperating." He pauses in front of the cedar chest at the foot of the bed. "Besides, that couch will be a luxury after last night."

He smiles at his joke, but I won't be dissuaded. "I won't steal your bed. Please, I . . ." I look down at my hands; I can't believe I'm about to admit this. "I don't want to be alone." How pathetic.

I expect him to roll his eyes or laugh, but he only nods and kneels in front of the chest. He pulls blankets out, stacking them in a heap on the floor.

"No, not down there." I sit on the corner and pat the bed. "We can share. Really, I don't mind." Am I really begging him to come to bed with me?

He shakes his head and continues his work, spreading the blankets out on the hardwood. His face betrays nothing of his feelings. "I've slept on plenty of floors in my day."

We're both adults, this shouldn't be so weird. It's not like I've never shared a bed with a guy. I cross my arms. "I can't sleep knowing you're down there on the hard floor."

His eyes meet mine over the top of the chest, a thick comforter hugged in his arms. He sighs. "Very well, in the interest of mutual comfort, I assent." Was that a flicker of a smile or my imagination?

A few minutes later, we climb into bed fully clothed—as agreed upon. I face away from him and close my eyes. Sleeping in jeans—this should be fun. I guess I could have asked to borrow those hideous neon shorts I woke up in, but I'm not *that* desperate. I resist the urge to glance back at him in the dark. It's stupid really. We've confessed to liking each other, sort of, so what's the big deal? But that was before the basement. Before I was put on house arrest. Before he lied. But he tried to tell me in the atrium, and I shut him up. And that's the problem. I can't think straight around him. I can't allow myself to get wrapped up in this, in him. Things will get out of control. Sure it'll be great for a month or two, but then his true nature will slip out, and I'll discover he's just as bad as the others. He will let me down; that's what men do.

My belt digs into my hip and I shift. I should have taken it off. It's too late now; he'll hear the jingling and get the wrong idea. The bed creaks as he rolls over. Is he uncomfortable, too?

After what feels like an eternity staring into the dark, I can take it no longer. So what if he gets the wrong idea? "I can't sleep in jeans."

"I was just thinking the same." His voice isn't even a bit groggy. Had he been just lying in the dark too?

We both laugh.

"Okay, we'll take off our jeans, but it doesn't mean anything."

"Absolutely." I can almost hear him nod.

Blankets rustle, belts jingle, and clothing drops to the floor.

I flop back on my pillow with a contented sigh. "Much better. 'Night."

"Goodnight."

But still, I can only stare into the darkness; his closeness is distracting. Sleeping in the same bed was a bad idea. He's no more than an arm's length away, sans pants. My brain automatically leaps to sex. Jesus. I swallow hard. Sex will only complicate our already complicated situation, and when this ends badly—of course it will—it's not like I can just dump him and disappear. I'm a prisoner here. Sort of.

But what if it *doesn't* end badly? What if this time it's right? He's not like the others. He's perfect. My eyes snap open in the dark and my hands clamp down on the sheets. Of course he *seems* perfect. He read my mind. He knows what I want and everything I'm afraid of. He knows what to say, how to act to make me comfortable. Or maybe I'm overthinking everything. If only I were more like Lisa. She's free. She doesn't analyze the reason someone wants her; men are just her playthings, nothing to be taken seriously. It only has to get personal if I let it, right?

His breath is slow and calm in the dark, and I wonder if he's asleep. I can't resist peeking, and I turn toward him. His face is bright in the dark. Too late, I notice his eyes are open and he's looking back at me.

"Can't sleep?"

I roll back onto my back and stare up at the ceiling. "No."

"Give me your hand."

I shake my head, but my hand slides toward him, between the sheets, across the miles of bed separating us. It seems like forever before my fingers brush his side, warm and firm beneath the thin cotton of his shirt.

His hand closes over mine, and I hold my breath, forcing myself not to panic, not to sigh.

He turns my hand up on his chest and traces soft, slow circles on my palm. "My mother used to do this when I had trouble sleeping as a boy. It always relaxed me."

It is relaxing, and soon my mind quiets and my eyes close.

Chapter 10

I'm disoriented when I wake. I'd slept hard and had many strange and chaotic dreams. The details are already fading as I struggle to make sense of my surroundings, leaving me with vague feelings of terror and despair. Then I remember where I am. I'm in *his* bed, only I'm on the wrong side, and I'm alone. I yank on yesterday's jeans and hurry downstairs.

I find Ambrose in the library, sprawled out on the tiny love seat in a patch of watery late-morning sun. His back is propped against one arm, a book in his hands, his legs dangle over the opposite arm. I watch him from the doorway, breathing slow and quiet, mesmerized by the way the soft light glows along the angles of his jaw, his neck.

"Sleep well?" He closes the book with a thump and sits up.

My cheeks burn. How long had he known I was watching? "I guess. When did you get up?"

He waves me over and I sit next to him. "Early. I rarely sleep through the night, and I didn't want to disturb you."

I glance at his book. "*Dracula*? Really? Don't you feel weird reading that?"

He laughs. "Not at all. It's a wonderful bit of fiction. Have you read it?"

"A long time ago . . . well, long for me anyway. I mean—sorry." Yeah, rub it in.

"Don't be sorry. Age is just a number. It's only relevant when you're waiting for death." He taps the book's cover. "It makes me a bit nostalgic. It was a fascinating era."

"Sure, from a man's perspective."

"History has not been kind to women. It's a shame. It has been interesting to see the gradual shift throughout time. Much has changed in three centuries."

"Sometimes it doesn't seem like anything's changed at all."

He stares out the window, squinting against the sun that's momentarily peeked around a bank of ominous clouds. He shrugs slightly. "It's more apparent having lived through it, I suppose."

I study his face. The tension I saw yesterday, along his jaw, is still there, but it's deeper somehow, farther below the surface. "Do you ever get bored?"

His eyes meet mine. "I don't believe in boredom. There's always something to learn and observe."

"Like what? What are you interested in? Besides books, obviously."

"All sorts of things. History, music, botany—"

"Music? Do you play?"

"Some." His eyes flit to the far corner by the window, and I notice a music stand with a small case at its foot.

I clap like a giddy child, forgetting myself in my excitement. "Play something! Please?"

He looks away, shaking his head, bright patches of color blooming on his cheeks. He opens his mouth to respond, and a loud jangling sound echoes through the house. Ambrose's eyes widen for half a second, then he laughs. "Ah, the doorbell." He stands from the couch, clearly relieved at the distraction. "I sent for your things, I hope you don't mind. I figured you would want them."

"My things? What things?"

"From your apartment. I wasn't sure what you'd want, so I had the movers bring everything."

"My—you . . ." My outrage turns to mortification as I remember the state of my apartment. With each remembered detail, I want to sink farther into the couch. Rain-soggy clothes in the kitchen sink, books scattered everywhere, my collection of tea mugs abandoned half-full, left to clutter nearly every flat surface. They were probably all moldy by now. Why couldn't I keep it to one mug at a time? That won't be a problem in the future—my tea drinking days are over. I don't enjoy vomiting. How long until the thought of consuming blood sounds normal or appetizing? Forever.

"You're upset. I'm sorry. I thought this would make you feel more at home."

"No, it's not—"

The doorbell rings again, and now he looks irritated. "Let me—just one moment." He rushes from the room.

❀ ❀ ❀

An hour later, the contents of my life hardly fill one corner of his huge bedroom. The boxes make me uneasy, fragmented. It's childhood all over again. Mom packing the car while Dad's at work. Living out of boxes, sleeping on couches until he he'd find us—he always found us—and persuade Mom to come home. *It'll be different this time*, he'd say. *I'll quit drinking for good.*

I sit heavily on the bed and shut my eyes. It's the same, but not. For the first time my life is in boxes and I'm not running from someone: my father, exes . . . myself. It's like starting fresh, but I can't help wondering when I'll have to start running again. I shouldn't be worrying about this. I've been given a second chance, a new life. I should change, grow as a person, face my fears, but what if I can't? What if I'm doomed to repeat my past forever? Do I even deserve better?

The bed shifts slightly as Ambrose sits beside me. "What is it?" he asks, his voice soft.

I stare into his strange violet eyes—my eyes. I wish I knew what he saw in me. I can't comprehend what he'd want with someone so obviously broken. "I just . . . you've helped me, and I'm grateful, but why? People die all the time. Why me?"

His hand twitches toward me and drops to the bed. He looks down. "It's complicated."

I wait for him to say more, but he's quiet. Complicated how? Does he think I won't understand? I'm not stupid. I can feel myself withdrawing, shutting him out. I stand, not sure where I plan to go, but I certainly I don't want to sit here with him.

"Wait. Please. I want to answer your question. I just need to gather my thoughts."

I turn to look at him and realize I had it wrong. It's not that he thinks I wouldn't understand: he's embarrassed. I sit beside him, but not too close, and resist the urge to analyze his face as he works through his thoughts.

"In part, I feel responsible for what happened to you. I should have left with those men, followed them, but I was selfish and irresponsible—I stayed to flirt with you instead, compelling you to stay. I shouldn't have allowed you to leave alone."

"You used mind control on me?"

He winces, cheeks flushed. "I made you stay and dance with me . . . and tell me what you thought of me. I know it was wrong. I could have gone farther, and as horrible as it is to admit, I wanted to."

I feel a jolt of fear at his words. Is his telling me he could have made me do anything he wanted supposed to be comforting? Am I supposed to be amazed at his restraint? I don't know what scares me more, the fact that he violated my consent or that some twisted part of me is turned on by the idea, and I want to hate him for making me feel so conflicted. "So you felt sorry for me, or was it that you just felt guilty for taking advantage of me?" I struggle to keep my voice calm. "He was getting back at you, you know—that crew cut asshole. That's why he attacked me. None of this would have happened if you would've just minded your own business." Even as I say this, I know it's not true. I'm being petty. Crew Cut was a fucked up person. It could have been any woman for any reason. I was just in the wrong place at the wrong time.

"I'm disgusted with my behavior." His eyes squeeze shut, and he looks away. "I'm sorry."

"Then you can at least give me a reason."

His shoulders sag, and he gives a heavy, defeated sigh. "I feel foolish admitting this. We've only known each other a short while, but as cliché as it sounds, there's something between us. I can't explain it, but I know you feel it too. I can't get you out of my head. I've felt dead for ages, but you've made me care again."

I want to tell him he's full of shit, that I feel nothing for him, but he's seen inside my head. He'd know I was lying. But despite it all, I want to believe him. I want him.

His eyes meet mine, and his face is naked, so tragically beautiful. I want to kiss him. It shouldn't be a big deal, we've kissed before, but that was then, before I learned I couldn't leave. Before I was his prisoner.

He leans in, and I want to pull back but my body betrays me. My eyes slip closed in anticipation. And nothing. When I open my eyes, he's looking down at his lap, his hair hiding his face. He is silent, unmoving. Should I say something? I'm trying to decide what to say when he speaks.

"Earlier you asked me to play for you." His voice is soft and shy. "Do you still want to hear?"

For a moment I wonder if this is just a distraction, but I nod and follow him down to the library.

I take a seat on the couch, and he crosses to the music stand in the corner. He draws a deep breath, opens a small leather case, and delicately lifts out a violin. It's beautiful in a well-loved way, the dark varnish worn away along the back and neck, rough around the edges. He adjusts the bow and draws it across a block of resin, tunes the strings, then steps to the window. He stands there, his spine rigid as raindrops patter against the glass.

I lean forward, meaning to ask if he's okay, when he finally moves. He touches his bow to the strings softly, drawing out a high note that gradually swells, filling the room, growing in intensity. My scalp prickles, and I forget to breathe as he sways in time. The song is vaguely familiar, sweet and melancholy— as music should be—and as he plays, it's like each note is something secret that spills from inside him. His fingers glide and tremble along the violin's neck, and I find myself staring, my breath slow, wishing he would touch me like that. I wonder how his body would move against mine.

He's hardly been playing for a minute when someone speaks from the doorway.

"You two had better get ready, we're due at Prisca's soon."

The bow screeches tunelessly across the strings as Ambrose whips around, but he recovers his composure quickly.

It's Alan, standing just inside the door; he points to his watch. "It's nearly two now, but it's quite a long drive. Care to ride together?"

"Thank you, Alan, but we'll drive up separately." Ambrose wipes the violin down and returns it to the case, and I watch after it longingly, wishing he would play more.

Alan lingers as if he wants to say something more, his eyes cut to me for an instant before returning to Ambrose. "Do you still have the address?"

Ambrose flips the last clasp, and stands. "I haven't been in a long while, but I'm not completely out of touch."

"Right, of course. See both of you there, then." Alan turns to leave and glances back over his shoulder. "Don't hesitate to contact me if you run into any trouble."

Chapter 11

Prisca's house is bright and warm. Almost too warm. Two fireplaces roar in the large open ballroom, one on either end. The polished walnut floor reflects light from thousands of tiny bulbs studding intricate chandeliers. Hundreds of people mill around, laughing and talking, sipping what can only be blood from delicate champagne flutes.

Among the tuxes and jewel-toned gowns, Ambrose and I look out of place in our jeans. Not that anyone could notice, as we're practically hiding behind the billowy fabric draping the walls, which is fine by me. It's my personal goal to make it out of here without interacting with a soul.

Strangely, my hands aren't clammy, though my stomach is in its usual tangle of anxiety. But hey, I'm so winning at not looking homeless: I'm showered and wearing fresh clothes. Nothing like clean underwear to make a girl feel special.

I glance at Ambrose. He doesn't look thrilled.

"Were we supposed to dress up?" I ask, more to take my mind off the situation because the answer is a quite obvious *duh*, and I'm still upset about him lying to me. I'm not completely convinced he's being honest about any of this, but he's the only person between me and a room full of richly dressed strangers. That, and I have no clue where we are. Some sprawling suburb in Washington is all I know for certain. We might as well be on another planet.

Ambrose's eyes shift around the room as if he's trying to see everything at once. When he speaks, his voice is distracted. "I'm sorry, I should have offered. You could have borrowed some of Anne's formal wear." His eyes flick to mine and he tries a smile. "Are you disappointed?"

My lip curls at the word *formal*. It reminds me of the once-a-year family photos where we'd dress up and plaster over the dysfunction with fake smiles. Nothing to see here, just a normal family, move along. But the truth was there, hidden. It was in our eyes. If you stared too long you could see the anguish, like something rotting below the surface.

"I've upset you. Do you want to leave?" Ambrose's tone is a little too eager. From the way his eyes dart around like he expects the walls to close in, I suspect he's asking more for his own sake than mine.

"Are we even allowed to leave?"

He gives me a wan smile and returns to studying the crowd.

I nudge his arm. "Relax. If anyone should be nervous, it's me."

He sighs and forces his shoulders away from his ears. "I haven't seen some of these people in forever. There are so many."

"When was the last time you came?"

His mouth opens and closes again, his shoulders creep back up and he laughs. "Sometime in the fifties? I suppose it's been longer than I thought."

Laughing about it seems to calm him a bit, and he gives me a genuine smile. The knot in my gut eases slightly. But then I spot Giric across the room.

Ambrose, following my gaze, takes my hand. "Come. Let's get a drink."

After last night's late dinner, I don't feel particularly hungry, but it's a good distraction. We plunge into the crowd and make for the refreshment table along the far wall. Ambrose fills two glasses from what looks like a giant keg. Chilled blood comes out instead of beer.

I take the offered glass and sniff its contents. The smell awakens my hunger and it takes everything I have not to chug it on the spot. "Do I even want to know where—*who* this came from?"

He raises his glass to mine. "Ignorance is bliss."

"Well, I'll be damned if that doesn't look just like Ambrose," says a man approaching from our right. He looks about twenty, with broad shoulders and a wide, friendly face. The violet of his eyes makes a stunning contrast with his dark skin and tailored charcoal suit. "But it couldn't be. The Ambrose I know would never be out in public." The man looks down at me and his eyes widen comically. "And with a lady no less? What's this? I was only away a week!"

A petite blonde wearing a showy hunter green gown steps to the man's side and presses a glass into his hand. She can't be more than sixteen, though her eyes appear much older. There's a quiet sadness behind them, untouched by the good-humored smile on her delicate bow of a mouth. "Let him alone, William, or you're liable to send him dashing to the nearest library and we'll never see him about again."

I clutch my glass and smile bravely at the newcomers. After my encounter with Giric, every part of me is ready and willing to dash.

"I'm not so bad as that. I've been to gatherings before." Ambrose shrugs. "Once or twice. Welcome home, Will."

Will grins and opens his mouth, but the pretty blonde jabs him in the ribs. "Manners, William. Introductions." She extends a hand to me, her grip is firm and sure. "You must be Sasha. I hear you'll be staying with us. I'm Anne, and the oaf here is William. He's a good friend but rarely is he serious, or polite."

"Hey—"

Anne carries on, talking over Will. "It's a pleasure to meet you. I'm sorry to hear of your trouble with Giric."

Will leans in, cupping a hand around his mouth for dramatic effect. "Did he really lock you two in the cells and torture you?"

Anne gasps and smacks his arm. "William! You're such a child. You see what I have to put up with?" She smiles playfully.

His massive shoulders bunch up around his ears. "What?"

Ambrose laughs softly, barely audible over the din. "No one was tortured, but we did spend a rather dull period in the cells. I'll have to remember to stow some books down there."

"And extra light bulbs," I say.

"A torch or two, at the very least." Ambrose smiles, but his attention is on the crowd again.

Anne turns to me. "Well, then. You've met all of us, all except my husband, Cleis."

"No, Cleis popped in briefly," Ambrose says. "He stopped by yesterday looking for you. He said he won't be long and then the trip to Canada is a sure thing."

"Canada! I said anywhere *but* Canada. It's always one more thing. It's not like the world will end if he spends a week at home."

Will grins. "How do you know?"

Anne sighs heavily and her eyes cut to the nearest door as if she expects to see Cleis enter at any moment, a flash of concern creases her brow.

Will touches her shoulder, his face suddenly solemn. "He'll be fine. He always is."

Ambrose leans in, speaking softly "What is it? Has something happened?"

Will's eyes dart to Anne and back to Ambrose. "It's nothing to get riled up about. If it was, they'd be making a big stink about it by now. Cleis's team hasn't—"

A microphone squeals at the other end of the room where a striking, ebony-skinned woman with razor-sharp cheekbones has stepped up to a podium. This must be Prisca. She holds her hand up for silence. She doesn't have to wait long.

"Welcome. My apologies for the delay in getting started tonight. This was intended to be a night of celebration, but as a few of you know, one of our teams has failed to check in. That in itself isn't unheard of, but we've just now received an automated distress message. Regretfully, our fears have been confirmed. Three are missing: Dorran Ziel of Nevio's house, Cleis Regillensis of Alan's, and Beth Sykes of my own."

My arms prickle with goose bumps. The air is heavy, charged, and a gasp runs through the crowd. *Quaadah* is the word on everyone's lips. It's flung around the room like a grenade no one wants to hold. In front of me, Anne's spine is rigid, and her hand flashes to her throat.

Will squeezes her shoulder. "He'll make it out. He's been at this longer than any of us."

"They said that about Ecrin, too." Anne gives him a false smile that screams *I'm barely holding it together*.

Will winces and tries to draw her into a hug, but she pulls away. She sets her glass on the table beside her, and weaves briskly through the crowd, picking her way toward the exit with lurching steps. It seems like she'll break into a run at any moment. Heads turn, watching her go, their faces drawn. A moment later, Will pushes through after her.

At the podium, Prisca stands silently, her eyes tracking Anne and Will out the door. She takes a deep breath and presses on. "At present, we have few details. As a precaution, the following have been selected to investigate: Blanche Strom of Artemisia's house, Ada Medwin of Darius's, and Sasha Rigel of Alan's."

The rest of Prisca's words jumble in my head. I heard her wrong, she couldn't have meant me, right?

My eyes flick up to Ambrose. He stands, shoulders back, jaw set, his eyes locked on Prisca. My gut clenches. How can I be selected? I don't even know these people.

I spy Giric across the room, and a wide grin spreads across his face. He winks, waves—a flash of gaudy lace—and melts into the crowd.

A shard of ice lodges in my gut. Somehow, he did this.

The room is silent, the cheer from moments earlier sucked away. The crowd disperses, eyes a little too wide, mouths thin. Ambrose hasn't moved. He's staring at the now vacant podium, his drink forgotten in his fist. His face is blank; it's impossible to tell what he's thinking.

I place a tentative hand on his arm and he starts, sloshing the blood in his glass.

"What have I been selected for?" I ask.

He shakes his head. "Nothing. It's an error. They shouldn't even have your name. You're not trained yet."

Alan waves from across the room and rushes over. "What a disaster. I'm sorry about this, Sasha. I can't imagine how your name was selected. Never you worry, you'll not be going."

Although I have a feeling Giric had something to do with it, to say so out loud sounds paranoid, so I remain silent.

"I'll ask Will or—"

Ambrose places a hand on Alan's shoulder. "That's kind of you, Alan, but between this and all that's gone awry this past month, you've got your hands full. I'll go. It's past my time anyhow."

I whirl on Ambrose. "You can't leave me here with—" My mouth snaps shut.

"You'll be fine. Alan and William will be here for you."

"But why you? Can't someone else—"

"No. When you're drawn, only one from your own house can go in your stead. Anne's in no state, heads of house can't go, and William needs to stay here with Anne."

"You people have the stupidest rules! What about Giric?"

Ambrose laughs bitterly, shaking his head. "Even if he would, which he wouldn't, I couldn't do that to Blanche. She'd surely kill him."

"You say that like it's a bad thing."

Alan's mouth pulls into a stern line at my comment, then softens. "It's just a routine procedure. Low risk." His eyes flash to Ambrose, then back to me. I'm almost certain he's lying. "He'll only be gone a week—"

A thick-limbed woman with cropped hair, dressed in dark grey fatigues, butts in at Alan's side. "What's this about new blood on my team? Someone's sure botched this job." She speaks rapidly, her voice gravelly with a touch of a German accent. It pairs perfectly with her pinched and angry face.

Alan cocks an eyebrow at her. "There's no need to be rude, it's been sorted. Ambrose will be going instead, and—" His gaze shifts to the door at the opposite end of the room, and the furrow between his eyebrows deepens. "Please excuse me."

Alan pushes through the crowd. I look after him, but I can't tell what drew his attention.

The woman shrugs and clasps Ambrose's arm, shaking him firmly. "It's been ages since we last traveled together. Do you even remember how to hold a sword?" Her sour face brightens, but she's still terrifying. "I only tease, you know."

Ambrose's lips twitch, but his eyes are on the crowd. "I just want to find Cleis and return quickly."

"Ah, that we will, with a good team. I trained Ada myself."

Ambrose lays a hand on my shoulder. "Blanche, this is Sasha."

A thin, awkward smile plucks at her lips and fades. "Welcome. Forgive my outburst, I just can't do my duty and look after a pup, you understand?" She shrugs her broad shoulders. "It's rotten luck to be reborn at a time like this. War is coming."

War? What war? I'm not sure how to respond, instead my eyes sink to my glass. I miss my quiet, no-action life where other people were the biggest threat, not an alien race bent on genocide.

From the corner of my eye I notice Blanche glance at her watch then turn to Ambrose. "We'll pick you up at noon tomorrow. Be ready." She nods curtly and strides away without waiting for his response.

Ambrose sighs and looks down at me. "I'm sorry. Blanche can be . . . blunt."

Blunt doesn't even begin to cover it. The woman has the personality of a cheese grater, yet she's still better than Giric. I remember his wink from across the crowd. "Do you think Giric did this?"

His eyebrow arches. "Did what?"

"Got my name drawn. I saw him in the crowd, and he gave me this look like . . . I don't know. I think he's out to get me."

"The drawing is random. Although . . ." His jaw clenches and his eyes flash. "No, even if he figured a way, it would never work. Alan would never allow you to go unprepared, and Giric knows that."

I grab his arm. "Do you have to go? Can't you ask someone else? Please?" The desperation in my voice makes me want to puke, but I'm helpless to stop it.

"We all have to serve. It's like the military. Some volunteer and go every time, like Cleis and Blanche, usually William, too; the rest of us go when we're drawn."

"Come on. Even the military doesn't do the stupid draft anymore. Please, can't Will go?"

"He's already gone in my place dozens of times. He needs to stay with Anne." His jaw clenches, and I can tell his mind is set.

"You can stay with Anne." I know I should drop it and shut up while I still have a shred of dignity, but I can't. My fingers wrap around his arm and he covers my hand with his. I flinch even though his touch is gentle and his face calm. I expect his features to contort, that his gentle hand will ball into a fist. I wait to see the monster inside of him. I wait to see my father.

But his face doesn't change, and if my persistence bothers him, it doesn't show in his voice. "Anne and William are close; he's like a brother to her. She needs him here."

I stand taller, though I still only come to the top of his shoulder, and set my jaw. I hope I look strong and determined even as I struggle to ignore the desperate tears aching to form behind my eyes. "Then I volunteer, too." I can't stay here with all these strangers. With Giric.

He shakes his head. "It's not safe and—"

"But Alan said it's low risk. You can teach me. Please." And now I sound like my mother—how pathetic. Maybe I'm doomed to lead her life. There's no escape; I'm just like her.

"No. Stop this now, this isn't you." His voice is stern, but his hand is still soft on mine, and that's what I hate the most. I want him to hurt me so I can feel justified in hating him. So he can leave and I won't care. So I can pretend I feel nothing for him.

I pull my hand from his and take a step back. "You know nothing about me."

"I know you're smart and capable. You'll be fine." He holds a hand out to me, but I make no move to accept it. He sighs and rubs his eyes. "It is low risk, but there is always some risk. If something were to happen to you . . ." He takes my hands in his before I can react, and I don't pull away. "William will start your training while I'm away. You won't even miss me."

My eyes drop to the floor. I want to beg more, sure that if I could just say the right thing he might stay, and I hate myself for feeling so needy.

He lifts my chin. "You can do this. You're strong."

❉ ❉ ❉

Ambrose's enormous walk-in closet is comically devoid of clothes. There's a row of identical black jeans, another of black t-shirts, some with long sleeves, and a few button-down shirts. Below that are two pairs of boots, exactly like the ones he's wearing. The rest of the space is packed with books and old wooden crates. "I've never known anyone with a library in their closet."

"What?" Ambrose glances up from the backpack he's filling. The sight of it makes my stomach clench; soon he'll be gone, and we'll have squandered our remaining hours together, all because I'm too shy to ask for what I want. We've already kissed, I know he likes me. Why is it so hard? Just walk up and grab him.

I step into the doorway, lose my nerve and instead say the first thing that pops into my head. "Hey, look at that: All your blacks match." Yes, resort to rambling. Great plan.

He freezes in the process of tucking a shirt into his bag, his brow bunched. "My what?"

Was that confusion or annoyance on his face? "Never mind." I push off the doorframe and take a seat on the chest at the foot of the bed. The wood is smooth under my hands.

Frowning, he carefully folds another t-shirt and tucks it into his bag. "I had to fill this space somehow. I've never been one for fashion, and I detest shopping. I find something that fits, order several, and I'm done." He shrugs. "And black hides the bloodstains." He zips the bag—a heavy, final sound. He catches me watching and smiles, shutting the closet door behind him. "I should only be a week, two at most."

I stretch out on the bed like I don't care, mostly to avoid looking at him. Late morning light pours in through the windows, reminding me of the passing time. How much longer before he's gone? An hour? Less? He seems so relaxed about the whole thing, but I can't shake this suffocating feeling of impending doom.

I get a sense that I'm being watched, and raise my head to find him still standing by the closet, his bag hanging, forgotten, in one hand. There's a strange look on his face: a determined, hungry look. It's gone in an instant, but I'm sure it was there. I know that look well. I'm sure I've looked at him in exactly the same way. Then I realize the message I'm sending, lounging on his bed like this, it must look like an invitation. And maybe it is. This could be our last chance; he's leaving. It's low risk, so Alan says, but the look the two of them shared told a different story. I can't let fear dictate my love life forever, can I? I really don't want to sit up, especially after having spent yet another night of torturous, PG bed-sharing, but apparently the answer is yes.

Yes, I'm too scared to ask for what I want. To allow myself vulnerability. I drag myself to the edge of the bed, brain and body fighting the whole way.

Something must show on my face, or maybe he feels that sense of doom, the ticking clock, because he abandons his bag by the closet and joins me on the bed.

"I'll be back. This isn't goodbye."

His thigh is warm against mine, and I rush to distract myself. "What happened to the other woman who used to live here?"

His eyes meet mine. "Ecrin?"

I nod and return his gaze forcing myself to focus on his words instead of his soft lips, the warm press of his thigh.

He shrugs. "There's not much to tell. She just disappeared one day, but that was nothing new. She was prone to disappearing for days, sometimes weeks. No one went after her, or suspected anything was amiss until it was too late. We keep better track now; she was one of the reasons we started these search parties at the first sign of trouble."

"Is she dead?"

His shoulders creep up and he eases them back down. "After ten years, everyone assumes the worst."

"What was she like?" I don't want to look away as I ask; I don't want him to think I'm asking out of jealousy, because I'm not. Well, maybe I am, but only a little.

He shakes his head. "I seldom saw her. She was a lot like Cleis in that she was always preoccupied with the Quaadah. She and Cleis inspired each other to work harder. They pushed for more training and greater involvement in the fight for freedom. Her disappearance made Cleis even more fervent."

He falls silent, then that hungry look is back and an instant later, our lips press together, and his arms wrap around me, crushing me against his chest. I feel safe, I feel home—I wish I could touch him forever. Then Ambrose is nudging me back onto the pillows, his mouth soft and hot on mine as his body presses against me, warm between my thighs. A fire expands within me. This is what I need; it's all I need. It's a strange feeling, this need. It overrides the alarms and the fear, the urge to run.

My fingers creep beneath his shirt, forcing it up and over his head. A moment later my shirt joins his on the floor; hands and mouths greedily seek exposed flesh. His lips trail to my neck, and I shiver at the sharp sting as his teeth draw blood. I want to scream. I want him to never stop. I want him to drink me completely, and I'm shocked at the feeling of dependency. It's too much like a drug, and I'm helpless against it, against him. Am I losing myself? I'm not sure I care anymore. Maybe I'm better lost, better within him. It's not such a big deal, is it? So what if he breaks my heart; isn't that a fair price for the chance to feel? My cheeks burn and my hands shake as I clutch him tighter. His mouth finds mine again, salty with my blood.

There's a soft knock at the door, and he pulls away. *Please ignore it*, I want to scream. We can't possibly stop now. I want to tell him it's okay, that I don't want to pretend anymore—I don't want to hide. He can have me, all of me. I'll stay forever, whatever he wants, just don't leave. But the words won't come, and the moment fades. I'm shutting down, drawing back. My mind's already at work convincing me that this judgment lapse never happened, will never happen again, that this foray into feelings was nothing but a chemical reaction: there's no such thing as love.

The knock comes again, louder, and I dive for my shirt. Ambrose, already pulling on his own shirt, runs to get the door.

Will stands in the doorway. He looks Ambrose up and down, biting back a smile. "Blanche is here. The car's waiting."

Ambrose nods. "I'll be right down."

Will turns to leave, pauses, and turns back. "Your shirt's on backwards and inside out."

Ambrose glances down, makes an exasperated sound, and slams the door. Will's laughter floats in from the hall.

I try not to stare as Ambrose rights his shirt, smooth skin slipping across bone like warm silk. He turns toward me, his face alive with yearning. It seems like he's going to say something, but instead he gives me an apologetic smile, and grabbing his bag, he heads for the door.

I follow him out and down the stairs, trailing after him like an idiotic puppy, my feet moving numbly on the steps, my sappy thoughts battling cold logic and losing. We stop at the front door, and he stands there, eyes unfocused, spine straight.

He snatches my wrist, and his eyes burn with a desperate intensity. My heart flutters. I can't breathe.

"I will be back. I promise." His hand dips into my hair and his lips press to mine. Then the door opens with a rush of cool air and he's gone.

❖ ❖ ❖

I climb the stairs to his room, my eyes burn and itch. I won't cry. I can't. I hardly know him. Maybe it's because I feel stranded without him, trapped in this house, surrounded by strangers.

I shut the bedroom door and collapse on the bed—his bed—and hug a pillow to my chest. It smells like him, and each breath carves a space in my chest, making me hollow. I throw the pillow across the room and ball my hands into fists, focusing on the hot sting as my nails bite into my palms. *This* pain is real, not this imagined, ridiculous heartache.

My gaze falls on the boxes across the room, and I set to work unpacking my stuff, desperate for a distraction. I set up my ratty secondhand bookshelves and dresser. My mismatched furniture clashes horribly with his finer pieces, but there's nothing I can do about it.

My last box is stuffed with clothes, but my dresser is already at maximum capacity. I'll have to make some space in his closet-library. I pull open the closet door to find that Ambrose has already cleared me a space. It's a small gesture, but it makes my heart ache all over again.

I finish hanging everything and browse through his books. Most of them are bound in dark leather with foreign words embossed in gold on their spines. One stands out: its leather is a yellowed beige, and instead of gold lettering, the words are seared into the binding. I work it down from the shelf. It's heavy, the pages uneven. I trace the symbols on the cover, following the swooping lines and harsh angles along the smooth leather. The writing is odd, similar to Arabic, but rougher, less elegant.

I open to a marked page a quarter of the way through, breathing in aged leather and the dusty, almost salty scent of the glue and delicate paper. It's the smell of the public library. After school I'd hide there among the books until closing; anything to put off going home. I would've stayed there indefinitely, made a nest on top of the high shelves or in the alcove beneath the stairs.

I flip through the pages, the unfamiliar writing continues throughout, handwritten in a rust-colored ink that's smeared and faded in places. A separate hand, in a newer but still ancient black ink, has printed in the margins in yet another language. Greek?

I slip the book back into its space, and my eyes drift to the wooden crates on the top shelf, just out of reach. I know I should leave them—it's not polite to snoop through his stuff—

he snooped in my head, so it's only fair that I do some snooping of my own, right?

I drag the chair in from the bedroom and pull the first box down. My hand hesitates at the lid. I shouldn't . . . but he took the time to clear space for me, he would have hidden anything he didn't want me to see. I know I would have. My curiosity wins, and I open the box, revealing several bound books of varying sizes and an ancient, rusted tin with faded and illegible writing across the top in what might be French. I flip back the tin's lid exposing hundreds of photos, some old sepias, others black and white, many more in dull, washed-out color.

In one picture, a man with wild, curly hair stands with one arm around Anne and the other around Ambrose. Anne and Ambrose have easy smiles, but the man in the center—his name's Cleis, I recall—his is more than a smile, it's the embodiment of joy, and I can't help smiling myself. I put the picture back and take out another. In this one, Ambrose scowls at the photographer over the top of a book. The hollow spot in my chest aches.

I replace the photos and draw out the largest of the books. I open randomly and come to a charcoal portrait titled, *Cleis— September 1683*. I'm impressed, it's a good likeness, though the shading is a bit off. I flip to the back and find another drawing, this one titled *Thaddeus and Leander Durling—January 1684*. It's two young boys of about twelve or so. They share Ambrose's sharp cheekbones. Possibly his brothers? The rest of the book is filled with landscapes: places I've never heard of, buildings and houses that likely no longer exist.

I trade the sketchbook for a smaller book. It's a journal, and the first page is dated 26 July 1902.

We've returned to America—to stay this time, Cleis says. Both Anne and I are glad for it. I can say with some conviction, should I ever again see another ship, it will be too soon. Here's to a future with a more practical means of transport, perhaps by way of Godwin's gansas or Verne's space gun, or better yet, no travel whatsoever. I've had a lifetime of it, several really. Cleis insists that with someone to share it with I might feel differently. He and Anne are surely fortunate to have found each other. He is of the thought that there exists someone for everyone. How the lovesick do drivel.

I force myself to snap the book shut. I shouldn't be reading this. I cram it into the crate and work the lid in place. With the box stowed, I feel a little better, better still when I'm back in the bedroom with his thoughts sealed behind the closet door.

It's raining again, and fat raindrops slip down the window. The afternoon sun forces its way through a break in the dark clouds, tinting the room the dusty yellow of a fading bruise. I scoop up the pillow I launched earlier and flop to the bed with it cradled against my chest. It's hard to believe it's only been a few hours since he left. It feels like days. How did I grow so attached?

I shake my head; there's no use denying it. I've been attached from the moment I saw him, as lame as that sounds.

A steady buzzing pulls me from my thoughts, and after a moment of confusion, I realize it's my phone. I sit up and hold my breath, listening, trying to remember when I last saw it. The buzzing sounds muffled and far away. When did I last use it? The bar when I called Ambrose.

I leap off the bed, my heart thudding, and rush to my bag in the corner. The ringing grows louder as I dig, but I only find my phone after everything from my bag is strewn across the room.

My breath catches when I see Lisa's name on the screen. She'll be angry. My finger hovers over decline, but at the last second, I squeeze my eyes shut and answer.

"There you are! I've been so worried." Her voice is loud, jarring.

I wince and hold the phone away from my ear, but her voice grows quiet. "We need to talk about . . . well, you know . . ."

I creep to the bed and ease onto the corner as if any sudden sound might cause her to explode. But it's weird—she doesn't sound mad. She sounds almost shy.

"Hello? Sasha?"

"Yeah, sorry." *Proceed with caution.* I take a deep breath. "I know I freaked you out. I'm sorry. I shouldn't—"

"No. It's okay. I mean, it's not like I haven't . . . you know . . . before, but I never thought—Well, I was surprised, is all." She laughs low and soft, a nervous laugh. "I never thought you, of all people . . ."

What the hell is she talking about? I know she's involved in some strange circles. Is it possible she knows about Hahmi? I bite my lip a little too hard and wince.

"I've been thinking a lot, and it all makes sense now." She's gaining confidence, speaking quickly. "You don't need to hide anymore. Over the past few days I've realized you're what I've been looking for."

Shit. She knows. "You didn't tell anyone, did you?"

Lisa laughs again—loud and almost flirty: the way she laughs when she's hanging on her flavor of the day. "What? You think I'm just gonna shout it from the rooftops? Hey! My friend's a lesbo, and I think I'm in love with her? Of course I haven't told anyone."

"Which frie—" Oh, she means me. I suck in a breath and press my fist against my lips to keep from giggling. Of all the possible ways Lisa could react, this is by far the most unexpected.

The confidence drains from her voice. "I need to see you."

I shut my eyes. Can I sway her over the phone? I cross my fingers. "You don't want to see me."

The line is silent and hope blooms in my chest, but her voice comes back smaller than ever. "I have to. Please? Tonight? You could come over or meet me at Vox . . . I can come to you."

It would have to be Vox, even though that means sneaking out. I'm not sure I can be trusted alone with her, not after last time, and she definitely can't come here. I take a deep breath and let it out. "Okay. Vox at eleven."

I hear her smile through the phone as we say goodbye. I hope I can fix this without hurting her.

I drop my phone back into my bag and there's a knock at the door. I open it to find Will standing in the hall, a sword slung over his shoulder. It looks strange paired with his designer jeans and button-down shirt—business casual meets fantasy warrior. I feel my eyes widen, and I can't help but smile. "Who are you supposed to be?"

He squints at me. "What do you mean? Ambrose asked me to train you." He shrugs the scabbard from his shoulder and holds it out to me.

I glance at the sword in his hand. "What? With that? We're supposed to fight aliens with swords?"

He shrugs and he gets this annoyed, *this isn't going to go well* look in his eye. "It may be archaic, but it's effective. The Quaadah are much like us: hard to kill, but decapitation slows them down. They're as good as dead until the head is reattached. The same is true for us."

My hand creeps to my throat and I swallow hard. "Reattached? We can survive that?"

He nods, grinning. "They used to call it Purgatory. Break the law and you'd be decapitated. But that's not even the worst of it. It's said the longer you spend in Purgatory, the worse the revival. The feeling is similar to the pins and needles when a limb falls asleep, only it's all over your body and it lasts hours, sometimes days."

I cringe. "That's horrible!"

"It's what they tell the young ones to keep them in line," he says with a shrug and holds the sword out again. "So, feel up for some training?"

It has to be better than moping around worrying about Ambrose. I take the sword.

"Leave that one here. It's for later. Today we'll use training swords. We practice in the atrium."

I lean the sword against my bookshelf and follow him downstairs to the mudroom. He pulls two rustic-looking swords from the umbrella stand by the door and steps out onto a patch of grass off the pebble path.

Rain drizzles down the glass walls, but inside it's dry and the air is sweet and lemony with magnolia. I glance at the flowering tree down the path where I sat with Ambrose. It already feels like another lifetime.

Will snaps his fingers to get my attention. "We'll train every day at two. Make sure you're ready. We have a lot of ground to cover. Let's begin. Sword up. Dominant hand on top, the other beneath. Like so. Good—just bit higher. That's it."

I mimic his stance, trying to keep up with his instructions, but I feel ridiculous, and I drop my arms. "Do we have to use swords? Can't we shoot their heads off or blow them up or something?"

He frowns. "You young Hahmi think you have everything figured out. These ways may be old, but that doesn't mean they don't work. The limb has to be severed, or in this case, the head. It can't heal if it's not attached."

"What about flamethrowers, grenades, rocket launchers . . ."

He shuts his eyes and continues as if I never interrupted. "When you attack, your dominant hand guides the blade, and the other controls the force. Try a few swings. Aim at my sword. Don't worry, you won't hit me."

I raise the dented blade, holding it as he instructed. It should be heavy but it feels light, but horribly unbalanced.

"Just a little higher here." He makes a minor adjustment to my form, nudging my elbow. "Good, hold right there. Now, eyes on the target and strike."

I focus and swing hard, connecting with his sword, and it clangs loudly, sending vibrations up my arm.

"Again. Put your whole body into it. Try to hit the same place each time."

I throw my weight into another blow.

"Good. Keep going."

I swing again and again. Soon I gain more control, and my hits begin to land closer together.

"Stop. Good. Now, if I were a Quaadah, you would need to jump to reach my neck. Try something like this." He jumps, sweeping his sword in a smooth arc.

I copy his movement, using his height as a guide.

"That's it. Don't stop."

After what seems like forever, he calls a halt. My legs are jittery from jumping, and the sword has gained ten pounds. If I were still human, I'd be too exhausted to move. This life has its perks.

"All right, one last lesson before we lose the light." He holds his sword over his shoulder, blocking his neck and head. "Jump and hit my sword. Aim for my neck."

"Seriously? What if I hit you?"

"That would hurt, so don't miss."

"Right. No pressure." I focus on his sword, and his neck beyond it, willing myself to aim true. My legs want to shake from exertion, but I force them to remain still. I jump, and my sword connects hard, throwing me off balance.

In a flash, Will is at my side, righting me before I fall. He's so quick; my movements must seem slow and childish. It's a wonder he keeps a straight face. I probably couldn't hurt him if I tried.

A cold fear settles in my stomach. Is Giric this good? Would I be able to fight him if I had to?

"Excellent, but work on that landing. Try a few more times."

I stand with renewed purpose, Will resumes his defense, and I attack. Each time I see Giric's smug face. I pretend the clang of metal is Giric's screams.

Chapter 12

Downtown is bright and crowded despite the chill. People stagger from bar to bar, the end of the week drawing them out to warm themselves with booze and company. I feel a little guilty for leaving the house on my own, but meeting with Lisa will be awkward enough without having to work in an excuse for Will, my ensure-Sasha-doesn't-slaughter-all-humanity babysitter.

I guess I could have told her he's my new boyfriend, but she wouldn't buy it. I haven't dated in over a year, and suddenly she sees me with two guys in one week? Nope. I could have said he's my brother. Yes, he's black—different mother. Oh, and I've never mentioned him before until now, but we're super close. Surprise!

But none of that matters, I can't tell Will anyway, as far as he, and everyone else, knows, I haven't been away from the house since losing my humanity, and it's going to stay that way. I don't even want to think about how much shit Ambrose and I would get in for that. No. I made the right choice. I'll be quick. Nobody will even know I'm gone.

I wind deeper into downtown, toward Vox, dipping into the minds around me, stealing glimpses into lives, witnessing secret thoughts hidden behind anonymous eyes. It was hard the first few times, but now it's like breathing, it's almost harder not to. I guess I shouldn't have been so angry with Ambrose for spying.

A group of women pass by, clinging to each other as they stumble along in heels ill-suited for walking. Their high-pitched laughter trails after them like bad perfume. I almost roll my eyes, but then I catch a glimpse of their pain, the insecurities that drive their behavior. For the first time, I don't view them as an other. Hearing their thoughts makes it hard to see them and judge. I never used to believe it, but we really are all alike. We harbor similar fears and hopes, despite the difference in our outward display to the world.

I can't stand the sadness that radiates from them, and an overwhelming urge to help swells inside me. How ironic that in losing my humanity, I've become more human. I jog after them and slide to a stop in front of them. One woman opens her mouth to speak, her pouty lips coated in a thick layer of pink gloss that glistens in the streetlights.

I raise my hand. "Shh, listen. You are all intelligent. You have your own power, and you are worthy of respect from yourself and others. Use your actions to inspire good in the world."

They stare at me, their mouths halfway open. A look of quiet wonder passes over their faces, as if they've solved a great mystery. I brush past them, continuing in the direction I'd been heading. I don't know if my words will improve their lives, but I desperately hope so.

Vox's neon sign flashes barely two blocks away, and my stomach bunches into knots at the thought of facing Lisa. It'll be easy: before she says a word, I'll just make her forget her feelings for me . . . or accidentally fry her brain and make her forget everything. No pressure.

The muffled bass grows louder with each step, and then the man at the door is asking for my ID. "You already saw it," I whisper.

He nods, and I brush past.

Right away I spot Dave, slumped on a stool at the bar, but Lisa's not with him. A quick scan of the teeming dance floor and make out nooks fails to turn her up. I take the stool next to Dave. With his low-cut vest—no undershirt, ample chest hair—and unruly sideburns he looks like a rockabilly boy band reject. He's got a broody look on his gaunt face. It looks like he's about to cry. Jesus. I don't have time for this. "Hey. Tell me where Lisa is."

He hunches his shoulders; his eyes never budge from his glass. "Outside with that dick she's been fucking."

Which one? I want to ask, but at that moment, his mind opens to me, a flood of self-pity and doubt. He loves Lisa, but he'll never tell her. He's afraid she'll laugh at him, so he pretends he doesn't care for her—that all he wants is a fuck buddy.

I touch his shoulder; thankfully his skin is cool and dry. "Tell her how you feel." I stand to leave but turn back. "Oh, and lose the sideburns. Lisa hates them." She *so* owes me.

I slip back outside. Several people are smoking under an awning a few doors down, but Lisa isn't among them. I jog around to the back of the building and spot a man in the shadows. Someone is pressed between him and the wall, and his fist is twisted in familiar blonde hair. It's Lisa. She flails against him, trying to break free.

Her fear threatens to invade my mind, but my anger rises to cut it off before it can take root. I charge, and my fist connects with the man's head a lot harder than I intend. He utters a sharp cry and crumples to the ground.

Lisa gapes at me, mascara streaking down her cheeks in black rivulets. "Jesus! You—" Her voice hitches. She tugs at the hem of her skirt, which is hiked past her hips, and leans over the man on the ground. "I think you killed him."

I kneel and find his pulse. It's strong. "He'll be fine. What about you?"

She shrugs and sucks her lower lip, rubbing absently at the tear tracks on her cheeks. "I told him I didn't want to see him anymore, and he spazzed out."

She draws a long shuddery breath, and her thoughts engulf me like a black hole. I see her for the first time, a glimpse of a past similar to my own. I resist the temptation to go deeper. The sadness within her surprises me, the desperation and circular belief that she deserves to be hurt, craves it even. That it's the only way she can feel anything at all. The Lisa I know is a facade. The real Lisa is this fragile thing buried deep inside, hidden behind wide, wet eyes.

I clasp her shoulders, ignoring the call of her blood. "You don't deserve to be hurt," I whisper, smoothing her hair.

Her breath streams out in a heavy sigh and she sags in my arms for a moment. Then her arms slowly slip around my waist. Her shoulders shake and I stroke her hair as her tears fall hot against my neck.

At last, her tears stop, and she leans back only to rush forward again. Her lips lock on mine, frantic and fumbling.

At first, I'm too surprised to react. "Wait," I manage to squeak against her lips. I step back, gently holding her at arm's length. "I don't want to hurt you, but I'm only your friend."

"But in my room—"

I shake my head and hold her gaze. I can't tell her the truth, but I can make her forget. "Nothing happened. You only know me as a friend."

Her mouth parts, and she smiles awkwardly at me. "I'm sorry. What were you saying?" She laughs and looks down at my hands on her shoulders. "I thought you weren't a hugger."

I release her. "I'm definitely not. I was just telling you how Dave was crying his eyes out because he saw you leaving with that jerk." I point to the man on the ground.

"Oh my god! Tom!" She stoops down at his side.

I pull her back to her feet. "Tom had too much to drink. Forget about him."

Her eyes go hazy, and I'm about to snap my fingers to get her attention when I realize what I've done. Oops. I'll need to be more careful with commands.

Her eyes focus on me again and she grins. "I like this new you, hugging, gossiping about Dave. Anyway, go on. What did he say about me?"

"He wouldn't shut up about how much he loves you. It was disgusting. He even said he's going to shave his sideburns."

She raises an eyebrow. "We can't be talking about the same Dave. The only thing he loves *is* those damned sideburns." She scoffs. "His idea of love is telling me I'm his favorite fuck buddy."

"It's all a front. He isn't even seeing anyone else. He's afraid to tell you how he feels."

She laughs—a real laugh—and her cheeks flush. "He really told you this? Man, he must be trashed!"

I raise my right hand like I'm in court. "I'm not making it up. Go talk to him."

She sighs and rolls her eyes, but she's grinning. "How do I look?"

I right her bra strap and rub the black smudges from her cheeks. "Beautiful." I hug her. She smells like soap and crisp autumn leaves. I ignore that deeper scent, warm and flowing, softly rushing. Her thoughts are racing. She wants to believe me. She wonders if she could be happy with him, if she even deserves to be happy.

"You deserve to be happy. Think about everything that makes you sad, all the things that make you feel worthless. Forget it all. Be the hidden you. The real Lisa." The words are out before I can even consider the repercussions. Will this make her life better? Worse? Will she even be the same person? All I can say for sure is if our roles were reversed, I'd jump at the chance to forget my past. But it's too late for me. I'm stuck with my memories forever, or at least until the Quaadah kill us all.

She blinks groggily, then her whole face brightens and she looks younger. Innocent. I'm envious of that innocence. What would it be like to start over with a clean slate? What would it be like to forget all the pain in my life? To be free to trust? A snide part of me whispers, *to trust is to invite pain.* I force the thought away and wave as Lisa disappears around the corner.

Tom groans and twitches at my feet. I don't recognize him, but then again, Lisa's relationships are always in flux. Who knows where she picked this one up. Prying into his mind, I see him for what he is. Not a killer or rapist like Crew Cut, but an insecure drunk with anger problems. I whisper in his ear and leave him lying there. When he wakes, he'll be a new man. Or maybe he'll just be completely brain dead.

❄ ❄ ❄

The crowds have thinned. Is it already so late? I reach for my phone to check the time, but of course I forgot it. I hurry along downtown streets, eager to get back to the house, but also

165

resenting that I have to. After my encounter a few days ago, the thought of walking alone down darkened streets should have reduced me to a sniveling child. But now it's pleasant, liberating. I feel invincible, powerful. I want to stay, perhaps find some prey, but there's no time for that.

Ahead, a steady stream of late night traffic walks along Burnside. My feet slow. I could lure someone back to the house. No one ever said I couldn't, so long as I don't lock them in the cells . . . but then again, luring someone back would prove I left. Damn.

Shrill laughter sounds from across the street. Two women hold each other, nearly toppling over. A large, well-dressed man is apparently relaying a funny story. I reach out to their minds, but I hear nothing. I push harder, and the man turns. His eyes center on me, and I realize it's Will.

I want to run, but it's too late. He's seen me.

"Sasha?" He dashes across the street. "What are you—you shouldn't be out alone."

My shoulders hunch and I study the sidewalk like a sulky teenager.

"Hey, don't get all worked up. It's just a one-time thing, right?"

I nod—the reformed child.

The two women make their way across the street.

"Sasha, this is Rebecca and Lan from Nevio's house. We were just deciding on dinner. Are you hungry?"

I nod.

"Have you fed at a club before, hon?" Rebecca asks. She's short and curvy with a mass of curly black hair.

I shake my head and swallow hard. "You kill people in public?"

Lan laughs. "No, sweet. Take a little here, a little there, like sex." She pinches Rebecca's bottom, and Rebecca squeals, twisting away.

I glance down at my feet. "I don't know if I can stop. I've never tried."

Will looks at me hard. "Ambrose has been teaching you to kill?"

I nod slowly, hoping I'm not getting Ambrose in trouble. "Only bad people. He says it's okay so long as we cover our tracks."

Will draws a deep breath. "Young Hahmi aren't allowed to kill. Especially on their own. He should've told you that."

"I've never done it on my own." Now I wish I had run. Why did Ambrose have to leave?

Will places a hand on my shoulder. "It's okay. Don't worry. I'll help keep you out of trouble."

"Come on. I'm starving," Rebecca says, tugging Lan's elbow. "Can we get country tonight?"

Lan's dark bobbed hair reflects the blue of a neon sign overhead. "Whatever you want, love." She kisses Rebecca's cheek and slips an arm around her plush waist, drawing her closer. She glances over her shoulder. "Does that work for you two?"

Will shrugs. "Anything close is fine by me."

Rebecca's curls bounce as she walks. "Country it is. There's a club a few blocks from here."

Headlights splash across us as a large black van races toward the intersection ahead. It swerves, nearly hitting the curb, before straightening again.

"Drunks." I shake my head, rubbing absently at an ache in my left wrist. I'm about to push my sleeve back to investigate when the van's engine revs loudly. The light at the intersection flashes yellow, but the van doesn't slow. It shoots through as the light blinks red. The headlights swell and as the van roars closer, careening straight for us.

It's like I'm pinned between the headlights. I can't move. "I don't think they're going to stop."

"Watch out!" Will yells, jerking me back.

Lan shoves Rebecca aside and manages to leap out of the way. The van hops the curb, and the undercarriage makes a horrible scraping crunch as the van skids to a halt, half on the sidewalk, half in the street. I break away from Will and take a step toward the van, shielding my eyes against the brilliant glare of the headlights.

Lan approaches the passenger side, her own hand raised as she peers through the tinted windshield. "You okay in there?"

There's no answer from inside the van. Lan and Rebecca step closer. I start after them but Will holds me back.

He sniffs the air like a cat. "We should leave." His voice is hardly more than a whisper.

Rebecca flaps a hand at him, and she and Lan slip closer.

They both freeze, and Lan's jaw drops. "No—" She stumbles backward, crashing into Rebecca. "No. No. No," Lan whispers, her voice cracking.

The doors fly open with a metallic squeal. Behind me, Will curses as six bald figures emerge. Their long white coats cover everything except their faces and fingertips. And their eyes—the whole eye—glow bright violet.

I hate that color. My wrist is itching again. I stare at them, transfixed, my insides like water as my confidence drains. I'm all too aware of how fragile, how weak, how totally unprepared I am.

"Run!" Will yells. He yanks me around by the back of my coat, propelling me in front of him.

"What about the others?" I scream, but the wind snatches away my words. I risk a glance behind me and see Lan and

Rebecca running in the opposite direction. Three of the pale figures pursue them, and the other three are coming after us and closing fast.

Panic nests in my stomach, and I stumble after Will on resentful legs. I want to sink to the ground and bury my face. As if hearing my thoughts, Will's massive hand clamps on my wrist. Distantly I hear, but I don't feel, the crunch as my bones break beneath his grip. He drags me, forcing me to move faster. We whip around a corner, he skids to a stop, and I crash into his back.

"What are you do—"

He tosses me over his shoulder like I'm nothing more than a doll. My stomach slams down on his shoulder, knocking the breath from my lungs. Then the ground falls away as he scales the side of the building.

Seconds later, he sets me down on the roof and drops to a squat, tugging me down beside him.

I gawk at him as he peers over the edge. My mouth is hanging open, and I force it shut. "You just climbed—Ah!" My left wrist pulses and throbs as the bones mend and I hug it against my chest.

"You okay?"

I flex my hand and glance up at Will, but he's still looking over the edge. "Yeah. Did we lose them?"

"Not likely."

As if on cue, footfalls echo from below. Will curses under his breath and helps me up. "We have to keep moving."

Somewhere behind us, a chilling scream pierces the darkness. Was that Rebecca or Lan? Just moments ago we were all fine. Laughing and talking. Now . . . I shudder, my knees buckle, and I fall hard, skinning my palm on the gritty roof; I hardly feel it. All I can see are their horrible, cold eyes. The thought of moving makes me shake. I'm going to be sick. If I just curl up here, I'll be safe. Invisible.

Will squats in front of me, and his hands fall on my shoulders. "They'll figure out where we are before long. Come on, just a little farther and this will all be over."

"Over?" I shake my head. "It won't be over! They'll always be after us." I didn't realize it until now, but I'd wanted so much for the Quaadah to be nothing but a myth. I'd hoped that Ambrose wasn't serious, that maybe this was all a stupid joke, some elaborate hazing ritual.

Will pulls me to my feet. "You're too young to think like that. There's always hope. Come on. A little farther. My car is just a few blocks away."

I force my legs to stop shaking, and I let him lead me to the roof's edge.

"Impromptu training. Whatever you do, don't look down." He runs and leaps to the next building, and somehow, I follow.

❈ ❈ ❈

Will is silent the whole way home. It's almost two in the morning by the time we return. The house is dark, but Will doesn't turn on any lights. I want to ask him about the Quaadah, about Rebecca and Lan, but I can tell by the set of his jaw that now is not the time. He mumbles good night and trudges down the hall, leaving me alone in the foyer.

I start up the stairs. As I reach the landing, a shadow peels back from the wall, and Giric steps from the gloom. The doorway at the end of the hall stands dark and open behind him. He's been waiting. He glares at me as I shuffle past.

"Take care, Sasha," he whispers, then he slips back to his room and shuts the door with a soft snick.

Goose bumps stipple my skin. Is he threatening me? I dart to my room and lock the door behind me. The heavy wood feels flimsy against my back. How long would it take him to break in? A minute? Two? My hand creeps to my throat. I can almost feel his blade on my skin.

Well, I won't make it easy for him. I open the chest at the foot of the bed, remove one of the comforters, and stuff it under the blankets on the bed, shaping it into something resembling a sleeping form. Satisfied, I toss one of the pillows and another blanket from the chest into the closet.

My eye falls on the sword in its plain black scabbard, leaning against my bookcase. I sling it over my shoulder and barricade myself in the closet. I sit in the dark, huddled in a nest of blankets, the door barred with a chair, naked steel in my lap. I wait, fighting sleep.

Chapter 13

Ambrose shifts next to me on the giant bed, and I turn in the dark. His back is to me. One shoulder peeks out over the comforter, a pale moon in the darkness. I'm a little hurt he didn't wake me when he came in, but I'm glad he's back. I slip closer, but he doesn't stir. He's tired, and I shouldn't disturb him, but I can't stop myself. I stretch across the expanse of bed; my fingers graze his skin. He springs up, seizing my wrist, his fingers dig into my flesh. I squeak and try to pull from his grip, but he holds firm. He yanks me closer and pins me against the pillows.

His eyes are still closed. Is he sleeping? I reach for his cheek and he snatches my hand, then both my arms are jerked over my head. Panic fills my chest and I struggle to calm my breath. I'm okay. He doesn't mean to hurt me. He's just dreaming.

My wrists ache in his grasp. "Ow! Ambrose! Wake up, it's me!" I try to scream, but my voice won't rise above a hoarse whisper.

His face is calm, his eyes remain closed.

"Stop! You're hurting me! Wake up!" Still my throat won't work, and he doesn't hear. I thrash under him, trying to buck him off, but he's too strong. At last, his eyes snap open, but they're not his: they glow, fully violet, like *theirs*. He squeezes my wrists tighter, and I fight harder, struggling to pull from his grasp. I want to close my eyes, but I can't. I can't look away.

His face looms over mine. "Your life is but a borrowed thing. We will have it back," he whispers, only it isn't his voice; it's cold and horrible, full of detached loathing and somehow familiar. Where have I heard it before? A dream?—A van; someone's inside, a flash of red, then violet. Everything's violet.

My heart pounds in my ears, and I twist beneath Ambrose, desperate to get away from that voice, those eyes. His face looms over mine, and then his eyes are melting, oozing down his cheeks in violet rivers. *That's how they get you*, and I know if the fluid touches me I'll be lost forever.

❀ ❀ ❀

My screams wake me, and I flail in the dark, smacking my head on something hard—a shelf? I'm in the closet, alone. Ambrose is still gone. Someone is pounding on the bedroom door. I untangle myself from the comforter and stumble into the bright room. Too bright; it has to be noon at least. How did I sleep so late?

"Sasha! You in there?" Will says through the door.

I pull the door open. "What's going on?" My voice sounds startled and froggy with sleep.

He stares at me like I'm missing something.

"What?"

"Training at two?"

I groan.

❧ ❧ ❧

"Try again."

I rub my throbbing cheek and scowl at the sunlight glinting off the glass of the atrium. The first sunny day all winter, and I have to spend it getting punched in the face by a giant. I can't help but assume this must be punishment for last night. I sigh and smooth the blindfold back over my eyes.

I try to sense him, but there's nothing, and once again his fist slams into my cheek. Lights flash in the darkness behind my eyes, but not the lights I'm supposed to see. Not the sensory energy field, or whatever he calls it—the shadow-self. Though why it's called a shadow when it's supposed to be neon light, I have no idea.

"Do you have to hit so hard?" I massage my cheek until the tingling stops.

"You won't learn unless it hurts."

Thanks, Dad. I lift my blindfold and glare at him with one eye. "I won't learn anyway. You're just pissing me off." I debate the effectiveness of telling him why a man saying shit like that to a woman is problematic.

"If you ever hope to survive an actual fight with the Quaadah, you need to learn."

"What are the odds of that? Once they get you it's over." In my mind, the van doors fly open. I shiver.

"Not always. I've killed my share."

I pull my blindfold down around my neck. "Really?"

He shrugs one massive shoulder. "I chopped their heads off anyway. They probably lived, but maybe not. And we survived last night, didn't we?"

"Barely." I see pale forms running after us, and I suppress a shudder. "What about the other two, your friends?"

His eyes cut away for an instant, and he brushes imaginary lint from his immaculate shirt before looking back at me. "They're fine. Don't worry about it. Right now you've got to train so next time, you'll be ready."

He's lying; I heard that scream. "So, they made it out okay?"

"Alan's taking care of it. Now, come on. Blindfold up. Focus. See with your mind."

"Will there be another search party?"

His jaw tenses. "Alan's handling it. That's all I can say. Now, focus. Please." He flaps a hand toward my face.

He's not going to budge. The blindfold is fitting as it seems I'm to be kept in the dark. I huff and pull the cloth back over my eyes. I try to focus, but Ambrose's face swims up, violet fluid spilling down his cheeks.

Will's fist slams into my jaw and a scream escapes my throat. My knees buckle, but hands seize me, righting me before I fall.

"Are you feeling okay? Maybe we should stop for today."

"Seriously?" I rip off the blindfold and throw it to the grass, barely resisting the urge to jump up and down on it like a tantrum-having toddler. "No! I'm not *feeling* okay." My voice hitches, and I take a deep breath, bunching my hands into fists. "We almost died last night—those women, they're dead. I know it, and you're acting like nothing happened! I just can't . . ."

His jaw clenches, then softens. "I know it's hard, but you can't dwell on it. We can't do anything for Rebecca and Lan— that's just the way it is. We shouldn't have been out unarmed. That was stupid." He touches my arm. "Come on, I know training is hard, and it isn't fun. We've all been through it. But believe me, you'll feel better knowing you can hold your own."

I remember the way Giric waited for me in the dark hall, like he knew what had happened. "What about other Hahmi?" I ask. "Do you ever have to fight each other? Like, I don't know . . . what if someone goes bad? They could be spying for the Quaadah."

"Sure, there are spats every now and again, but to kill one of our own is considered the highest crime. It's not common."

"What about threatening another Hahmi?"

Will crosses his arms over his broad chest. "Is this about Giric? Is he harassing you again?

Again? He never stopped. I nod.

"I wouldn't worry about him—he's all bark. Just sore about his demotion. It's been a long time coming, if you ask me. Power goes straight to his head."

"You don't think he could be a spy?"

"For the Quaadah?" Will laughs. "Not even Giric is that stupid. Why?"

I shrug. "That's just how it is in books."

His face cracks into a grin, he slaps his thigh, and howls with laughter. My cheeks grow warm. "You and Ambrose. It's no wonder he likes you. Peas in a pod. You both need to get out and experience real life more often. It's nothing like fiction."

He's right. It's stranger.

Chapter 14

The sunny weather of the past few days is once again replaced with grey gloom. It's almost a relief; the sun clashes with my disposition. I sit on the couch in the library, a book open, unread in my lap. I can't focus enough to read. It's like the words are in another language. My hands shake. I need blood, but I'm not about to leave the house looking for it like Will. He acts as if nothing happened. The whole thing hardly fazes him.

Every time I shut my eyes, the van doors fly open and creepy beings clamber out, the streetlights glaring off their luminescent white skin. Those weird, massive violet eyes. They're out there, waiting for me, searching. And I'm not ready. I'll never be.

"I thought I might find you in here."

I turn to find Alan in the doorway. How long has he been standing there?

"How are you holding up?" he asks, crossing to the couch.

"Fine," I lie.

He gives me a soft smile and gestures to the couch. "May I?"

I nod, and he sits.

He brightens and pats my knee. "William says your training is coming along."

I wince. We've been at it for three days, to no avail. "I can't get past the shadow-self thing."

"You will. It's the human part of us that makes that bit so difficult. We cling to our customary way of sensing the world, accepting its limitations without question. To master it, you must unlearn those limitations." His brow creases. "The shadow-self is naught but the mind's visual manifestation of the senses. It's the key to surviving against the Quaadah."

"Have you killed them?"

"I've faced a fair few." He gazes out the large picture window, his thick eyebrows knitting together, forming that deep yet endearing worry line. "War is coming. You must do all you can to prepare. We all must." Alan's voice softens, and his eyes return to mine. "Have you seen Giric lately?"

I want to tell him about how Giric threatened me, how I'm sure he's up to something evil. But then I remember how Will laughed at my concerns. Will would know better than I, wouldn't he? I just shake my head.

He looks as if he's going to say something more, but he changes his mind. "You look a bit peckish. Have you fed?"

He can tell? I spent forever concealing the dark circles under my eyes, then further masked them with heavy eyeliner. I look like an emo panda. "Not yet. I will later." I resist the urge to look away. I don't want to lie to Alan; he's so kind and gentle. He's the man I wish my father would have been, but I can't tell him I've hardly slept since Ambrose left, and that when I do, my dreams are poisoned by violet eyes and grasping hands. I can't admit that the only place I feel safe is here in this house, and even that is shaky with Giric glowering at me from the shadows. I've heard the whispered reports—eight more have gone missing in the last three days. Each new name aches like an elusive splinter lodged beneath my skin, sinking deeper, becoming infected, festering. I won't end up on that list. I'm never leaving the house again.

Alan smiles in a way that suggests he's on to me, or maybe it's just my guilty conscience. "See that you do. You must keep up your strength. But do feed away from the house. William will be happy to escort you." He pushes back his sleeve to check his watch. "I must be going. So much to do, so little time." He stands and glances down at me. "I'm sure Ambrose told you, but the neighbors are off limits. We must keep up appearances."

My heart leaps at Ambrose's name. "Have you heard from him?"

"They haven't found anything yet, but I'll tell him you send your love next time he checks in." He pats my arm and leaves the room.

My love? Love is an odd concept; one I don't fully believe in or understand. I can define hate, lust, fear, contentment even, but can two people really love each other? It's an impossible ideal. To be true it has to be unconditional, honest, earned— but nothing is unconditional, no two people can ever be completely honest with each other, and anything earned can be lost. Still, I feel something for Ambrose. More than I want to— more than I'm comfortable with. I hardly know him. But who knows how I'll feel once I discover who he truly is behind his seemingly perfect mask. I remember his journals up in his closet and quickly push the thought away. Spying in his journals won't bring him any closer.

My eyes drop to the book in my lap, and I groan. It isn't even in English. I stand to find another, and the room spins. I grab the arm of the couch. It's not the hunger—I just stood too quickly. My mind buys the lie, and after a moment, the spell passes.

I return the book to the table where I found it and survey the shelves. The number of books is overwhelming, almost panic-inducing in a weird way, and I find myself paralyzed by the options. I slide the track ladder all the way over behind the door and run a finger through the dust on the nearest shelf. Someone's been slacking on the dusting.

Footsteps echo in the hall, and Giric's voice floats in from the foyer. I crouch behind the door.

"Forgive me, my mind has been elsewhere these past few days . . . I know, it's no excuse . . . but, please . . . Of course, I'll be ready . . ." Giric's voice fades as he climbs the stairs.

I creep into the foyer, ignoring the pulsing lights swirling at the edge of my vision. He's up to something, I'm sure of it. I pad up after him and pause in the hallway. Giric's muffled voice drifts from under his closed door. I sneak closer and press my ear to the cool wood.

"I have, and I've been patient, but when? I am failing to see the mutual benefit in this." He is quiet for a moment, and I draw back, afraid his call is over and he'll open the door, but his voice has only dropped to a whisper. I press my ear closer shutting my eyes, but I still can't hear.

Then his footsteps are rushing toward the door. My heart leaps. There's no time to run. My spine snaps straight, and on impulse, I raise my fist as if I'm about to knock.

The door flies open and he nearly crashes into me. His eyes widen, then narrow to menacing slits. "What are you doing?"

I swallow hard, searching for something to say. "I— I . . . Alan's looking for you. I just came to let you know." My voice sounds weak and stupid. Can he tell I'm lying?

Giric's eyes widen for a moment, then his face locks down and he gazes down his nose at me, his lip curling slightly. "Well,

Alan will have to wait. I have business to attend to. Now, if you'll excuse me."

He steps out, locks his door, and pushes past me. He rushes down the stairs, a moment later, keys jingle faintly in the mudroom, and the garage door slams.

I sag against the wall and let out a shaky breath. What was I thinking? But even as I chide myself, my eyes drop to the lock. I could have that open in less than a minute—have a quick look around. It's not a good idea. I should mind my own business and stay out of his way. But I remember the look in his eyes, his whispered threats. If I can get something on him maybe Alan will get rid of him.

I race to the opposite end of the hall and throw open the door to the tiny terrace just in time to see taillights flash on the drive and disappear around the corner. I force myself to wait, allowing my heart rate to return to normal, listening to make sure he isn't coming back, before retrieving my lock picks from my underwear drawer.

It seems I haven't forgotten everything from my delinquent youth. In less than a minute, the lock gives and I'm inside with the door closed behind me. I should be worried: I'm slipping back into old habits, snooping, sneaking out, picking locks. How long before I start shoplifting? "Shut up," I mutter under my breath.

I make my way across the room in near darkness and peer out the heavily draped windows. Outside, nothing moves; it's dark and quiet. I let the drapes fall back and flip on the light. Something stinks. I didn't notice it at first, it's faint, but it definitely smells like something's rotting. I look around for the source. Nothing seems amiss. The room is tidy with a layout similar to Ambrose's, except the bathroom and closet are together along the north wall instead of on opposite sides. A mahogany desk dominates one corner, and a massive, curtained bed is pushed against the east wall alongside the farthest window.

I cross to the desk and settle into the velvet chair. Aside from a small brass and green glass lamp, he keeps nothing on the desk's pristine, polished surface. I pull the nearest drawer and it slides out smoothly. Inside is a mess, a striking contrast to the cleanliness of the room. Pens, paperclips, and other random objects are scattered throughout. At the back, there's a yellow memo pad with an address scrawled in an elegant hand. Maybe the address is important? I roll up my sleeve and copy it onto my wrist. I dig through the jumble, hoping to find something incriminating. There's a gold ring inscribed with foreign lettering, a bundle of keys, and a flash of white—a folded picture. I fish it out and unfold it, revealing Ambrose and Giric standing together. Someone else was in the photo, too, but they've been carefully cut out, only a hint of an arm remains. Ambrose is smiling, his face angled at the missing third party.

Does Giric have a thing for Ambrose? That would explain why he's being such a jerk. Either way, it's quite clear Ambrose doesn't reciprocate. I desperately want to ball the picture up and throw it away, but I return it to the drawer.

I search through the other drawers but find nothing of interest. As I close the last drawer, I catch another whiff of that putrid smell. It's awful, like potpourri mixed with rancid meat. I stand, sniffing the air. It seems to be coming from his bed. The thick curtains glower at me, taunting, like the flaps of a macabre circus tent. See the wonders within, they seem to say.

I don't want to, but I pull back the curtain. Pure, undiluted stench rolls over me. Then I see him. A man stares back at me with glassy grey eyes. I stifle a scream. The man looks remarkably similar to Ambrose, if you don't look too closely:

thin, pale, long dark hair. He's been dead several days at least, but he's tucked beneath the covers as if he's only sleeping.

I gag and back away. The curtain slips from my fingers, falling back to conceal the secret, but I can still feel his eyes. The smell intensifies, as if knowing its source makes it more potent. The room feels too hot, and that stench is seeping into me. I can taste it, and my stomach lurches. I have to get out. I switch off the light and lock the door behind me.

Back in Ambrose's room, my breath comes in shaky gasps. I can't get the dead man's eyes out of my head. Why didn't Giric change him? The answer is obvious, of course. Once he was Hahmi, Giric wouldn't have control over him. He couldn't use him as his personal sex slave or whatever. I don't want to think about the horrors that man endured. To be forced against your will is one thing, but to have no will at all. I shiver. It's too horrible. Horrible enough for Alan to get rid of Giric? Probably not. It only proves that he's is a disgusting jerk.

I push up my sleeve and study the address written on my arm. It's fairly close by, just on the other side of the river. I grab my phone from my dresser and tap the address into the map. It's a warehouse in the industrial district, not too far from my old apartment. If Giric is up to something, that would be the place to do it: low traffic, no residential neighbors. If I can catch him in the act, we'll all be safer. Or maybe I'm making a big deal out of nothing.

I drop to the bed and bury my face in my hands. Whatever I'm going to do, I'd better do it soon. But I need to feed first. It's been four days, and I'm weak. Not as weak as my first time, thankfully, but the dizziness is lurking just around the corner. Tomorrow. I'll handle everything in the morning.

❖ ❖ ❖

Headlamps splash across the warehouse. It's just a flash before they wink out, but it's enough to get her attention. This isn't a busy area, especially not this late. She settles her hood over her white-blonde hair and slips around the side of the building.

The wind is up, it whips at her robe and carries the noxious stench of hot metal from the refinery nearby. She sticks close to the building, within its shadow, searching for the source of the lights. As she nears the edge of the building, the wind surges, blowing back her hood. A figure moves in the dark, and she reaches for her hood a moment too late.

"Ecrin?" A man's voice, smooth, with a cultured English accent.

The robed woman starts, and the man who spoke steps from the shadows of the warehouse across the way—greying copper hair, dark, heavy brows.

Ecrin glances back toward the van—the warehouse door is still closed—then cuts across the road. "Hello, Alan." A pained smile stretches her lips, and she glances over her shoulder again. Alan's mouth falls open in reply, but she talks over him. "We have much to discuss, I know, but now isn't the time." She glances back again and something like fear colors her words. "I'm on the verge of a breakthrough. They mustn't see you. Leave now. I'll explain everything as soon as I can, but please, go now. Too much is at stake."

"Is it Giric? He's involved, isn't he?"

Her face betrays nothing. "It's under control."

Alan simply stares for a moment, his eyebrows drawn to nearly touching. Ecrin's hand twitches and her shoulders seem to quake as if fighting a chill, or maybe it's the wind in her robe.

"Please." She steps toward him, a desperate set to her mouth, but there's a tension in her: her hands, hidden in her sleeves, clench and unclench.

At last, Alan's face yields and he draws a long, slow breath. "You know where to find me." He stands there a moment longer, begins to lift his hand, lets it fall. His mouth quivers, then he turns and slips back into the shadows.

She waits, tucked against the rough brick. Distantly, an engine turns over. A moment later, the sound of the vehicle fades completely, leaving only the steady drone of the highway and the far-off clang of the factory up the road.

Chapter 15

I sink into the library couch and stare out the window. Rain falls from another gloomy afternoon sky. I still haven't fed. Last night I promised myself I would, but promises by night are like shadows: they dissolve in the light of day. Courage, too, is like those shadows. Just when I worked up the nerve, I learned that three more went missing overnight. Was Giric behind their disappearances? I hope not, I already feel bad about Rebecca and Lan, I couldn't handle it if I could have stopped it. How long before Ambrose's name winds up on that list? Or my own?

Someone passes by the window outside, a man running with his dog, both of them soaking wet in the downpour. I've seen this pair before; they probably live in the neighborhood. My mouth waters and I close my eyes.

I wish Ambrose would hurry. I'm almost positive Giric is trying to kill me. The look on his face when I returned that night said enough. He didn't expect me back. It seems far-fetched to suggest that Giric could be working for the Quaadah, but he's slimy enough that I could believe pretty much anything about him.

I remember the stench of death in his room. How can he stand it? Was he up there now, snuggled up against reeking cold flesh? Maybe I should tell Alan. But tell him what? That I broke into Giric's room?

The man and the dog pass by again, heading in the opposite direction. I consider running after them, luring the man in, just for a taste. I wouldn't be breaking the rules. Alan said no killing the neighbors, but I wouldn't kill him. I could stop.

I rise from the couch and cross to the window. My breath comes in ragged gasps, fogging the cold glass. I shut my eyes and grip the windowsill hard. Something stabs into my thumb and I jerk away. Bright blood leaks from the cut and warm, heavy droplets spill into my upturned palm.

I peer underneath the windowsill. The sharp tip of a nail sticks out, not much, just far enough. I look back at my thumb, where the flow continues. Why isn't it healing?

I bring my thumb to my mouth, and as the blood hits my tongue, an involuntary moan escapes my throat. My knees buckle and I collapse to the floor. I lean against the wall, lapping blood from my palm, the runner forgotten. I suck my thumb, tasting my own blood, my eyes slip closed, and my head falls back to rest on the wall. Bliss.

I don't know how much time passes, but at some point I hear someone calling my name. Am I dreaming? I try to open my eyelids, but they won't move. Whoever it is, whatever they want, doesn't matter. Only the blood is important. It's warm, and there's so much. So what if it has a strange taste. I'm so hungry. Whose blood is it? The running man? Did I go after him?

"Oh, no! Sasha. Stop!"

Someone is shaking me. The voice is feminine, but I can't see her. My eyes refuse to open. I groan and try to push her away, but her hand closes on my wrist, and my thumb is jerked from my mouth. The blood is gone. The fingers tighten, biting into my skin. "Ow! That hurts." My voice sounds brittle. Why can't I see?

At last my eyes open and a face appears as if through heavy fog. It's Anne. She holds my wrists tightly in her small, surprisingly strong hands. Blood runs down my thumb and oozes over her fingers. A pathetic whimper escapes me. I want that red warmth. I need it.

"What are you doing?" Anne's eyes are wild with panic. "You can't drink from yourself! It'll make you sick!"

"What?" I look around the room, my vision spins and distorts. "It was the runner," I mumble, more to myself than to her. Where did he go? I look down at my chest. My shirt, soaked with blood, clings to my skin.

Her fine, golden eyebrows slide together. "What runner?"

"There was a man outside. I think I killed him. Shit, Alan's going to be so mad. I was just so hungry. I only wanted a little . . ."

She draws back, smiling softly. "You didn't kill anyone; it was a hallucination. You've got blood poisoning." She releases my wrists and points to the fleshy part of my palm, just below my thumb where teeth marks are just starting to heal. "Drinking too much of your own blood will do that."

"My own?" I remember the cut on my thumb, how much it bled. "Oh . . ."

She looks at me knowingly. "How long since you last fed?"

I shrug. "I—I don't know." I'm not sure why I lie.

She narrows her eyes and cocks her head. "Judging by the rate at which these wounds are healing, I would say at least three or four days."

I nod and drop my head.

"Come on." She offers her hand, smeared with my blood. "Let's put you right."

She leads me to her bedroom, and I collapse into a chair, squeezing my eyes closed tightly as if that will keep the world from spinning: It doesn't. My head thrums. I hope I won't puke.

"I'll only be a moment." She slips out the door.

Sitting helps a bit. At least the spinning slows, so long as I don't close my eyes. Thick curtains have been drawn against the grey day, and warm light pools beneath red lampshades, splashing across the paintings and mounted poetry adorning her walls. The desk beside me holds several framed photos; most are yellowed black-and-whites, but there are a few color prints. I pick up the closest one, careful not to smear blood on the heavy, ornate frame. Anne stands centered, her face shining, her arms wrapped around Cleis who's smiling broadly with child-like dimples. They look perfect together.

The door opens and Anne hurries back in, her arms laden. She sets her load on the bed. "Here, drink this." She hands me a plastic pouch filled with dark liquid.

I hold the pouch to the dim light.

"It's blood, from my private stash." She smiles like she's sharing a secret. "One of the orderlies from the hospital up the way brings it for me." She fishes some scissors from her desk drawer and clips one of the protruding tubes. "There, see? Just like a straw."

I take a sip. It's cold, with a stale, preserved flavor, but it's still blood and I drink greedily. When I'm done, Anne exchanges the empty pouch for a damp towel and a fresh shirt, then crosses to the opposite side of the room to study a painting while I wipe the blood from my skin and change my shirt. I didn't realize just how weak I'd grown over the past few days. The blood helps, and as it works into me, I feel almost whole again.

I drop back into the chair and bunch the towel in my lap. "That's a nice photo of you two." I point to the framed photo in front of me.

She looks over her shoulder and nods, taking a seat at the desk. A sad smile tugs at her lips as she cradles the picture. "This one's from the nineteen seventies. A frightful decade by many standards, but we had a good time. It was quiet, peaceful." She sets the frame back on the desk.

"So you guys have been together for a long time, then?"

Anne nods and her delicate, shapely hands run over the smooth wood of a small oak box on the desktop. She pries off the lid and nudges the box toward me.

"What is it?" I ask, peering in at what appears to be a sliver of charred wood.

"The end of my human life."

I study the jagged fragment. "You died in a fire? I mean, obviously you didn't die, but—"

"Do you want to hear?"

I nod, leaning forward in my chair.

"It was 1745, not a week after harvest. I woke as the sun set to find myself bound to a post in the center of the fallow field at the edge of town. Nearly everyone from town was there, even the baker, sweet, elderly Mr. Farro. Just the previous morning, I'd stopped in for a loaf and asked after his ailing wife. His sad eyes found mine for a heartbeat before shifting away.

"It only took a moment to piece together what happened. My dress was tattered and bloody from the night prior. His blood. I never imagined a man could bleed so much. It's ironic that I thought that then, considering what I became, but I did. When I saw all the blood, I knew he was dead, and I didn't feel bad in the least.

"It was his widow who threw the first stone, screaming 'succubus' and 'witch'. Her aim was poor, and the stone lodged in the bundle of sticks at my feet, but her words hit and stung. Garrity, that was her name. Gertrude Garrity. Such an ugly name, it suited her. She'd always hated me. It was her husband: he had a wandering eye and adventurous hands, not to mention an inclination to take whatever struck his fancy. She was the one who gathered the crowd, telling them I'd used witchcraft to steal her husband, then murdered him as he slept.

"It was an outright lie; she and everyone knew it, but it had been a difficult year—the blight had taken hard to the wheat— and the crowd was eager for any excuse to vent their frustration. By the time I woke, she'd worked them into such a frenzy, that nothing I could say would change anything. I tried, of course, but it only made matters worse. You should have seen her face—so red, it was nearly purple.

"From there it was all downhill. Stones and insults abounded until someone shouted 'Burn her!' from the crowd, their voice so choked with fervor I couldn't be sure if it was a man or a woman. Within seconds the chant spread.

"It was then that Mr. Farro broke away and tottered back toward town, taking my last shred of hope with him. He would say nothing, but neither would he stay and watch. I know his words wouldn't have made a difference, but it still hurt.

"I looked upon my fellow townspeople anew. In that moment, I embraced certain death. If living meant being surrounded by their sort, so be it. Until I saw the flame. It came, dancing and bobbing over the sea of faces. The crowd parted to allow Mrs. Garrity through, a torch hoisted high over her head. I still remember the way the shadows writhed beneath her eyes; she was terrifying, a woman possessed. Wisps of her hair had worked free from her bun to swirl in the breeze in a shifting, glowing aura.

"I'd resolved to accept death. I wouldn't cry or scream, but as the hungry flame inched closer, I knew I would. Once, as a child, I burnt my hand on the stove. I remember the sizzle of flesh, the blisters that swelled and wept. I screamed then, and I would scream this time, too.

"Then I saw him—a stranger in the scowling sea—and everything fell away. He hardly seemed more than a boy, perhaps a few years older than I, but there was a hardness to him. He looked like a king. It was his straight nose and hard jaw. The dying sunlight played in his unruly curls.

"His eyes tracked the torch as it passed, then snapped to mine as if he sensed me watching. His eyes widened and his lips parted, and he pushed to the front in the widow's wake, moving like a spirit. I couldn't take my eyes from him. Even as the torch drew nearer, the roar of the crowd muted, and there was only him. And in him I felt calm, as if I could live a thousand lives within his eyes in one instant, as if I had lived those lives.

"The illusion shattered as Mrs. Garrity threw the torch. It tumbled end over end toward the bundle of sticks and chaff humped at my feet, catching fire to the dry kindling. Far away, the voices calling for my death changed to screams, frightened screams. Beyond the heat waves, the mob thrashed about like wheat in a gale. The flames climbed higher, banishing the chill air. There was so much smoke!

"Through the fire, I caught a blur of motion, and then the stranger from the crowd shared the pyre with me. For a moment I thought I died, and it hardly even hurt. Then a mouthful of smoke made me cough, and I knew I was still alive. A moment later, I was in his arms and safe on the ground. He asked if I could walk, but I could only nod. That was it for me— I knew in that moment I would love him forever.

"That's when I saw the bodies sprawled across the field. Rat-haired Mrs. Garrity lay supine, the toe of her boot smoldered mere inches from the flames, but she paid it no heed:

her throat had been ripped out, and a mist of blood peppered her face.

"At the sight of all the bodies, the blood, my mind turned to folklore. I asked what had happened, but he wouldn't answer. He tugged my arm, bidding me to follow, but I looked back, squinting into the gloom beyond the pyre. I saw two figures pursuing the fleeing townspeople. One by one the spectators died. They killed them all—everyone who was present. And the fire spread, leaping from corpse to corpse."

With a shrug, Anne replaces the lid on the cedar box and tucks it back in the corner of her desk. "I keep this as a reminder. As bad as things may get, I know I survived this."

I stare at her, gaping, and the silence stretches out between us. "Jesus . . . a whole town. The other two with Cleis—one of them was Ambrose, wasn't it?"

Her shoulders tense, and she takes a deep breath. "It's harsh, I know, but you mustn't think poorly of him. It was a different time. The world was different then."

I try to imagine what it would be like to keep drinking . . . person after person. I'm not sure what scares me more: the thought of doing it or that part of me would love it. That I wouldn't want to stop—that I wouldn't be able to. "It sounds so brutal. Couldn't they have mind-controlled them and told them to go home?"

"We can control humans to an extent, but mobs are different. Once they get worked up, it's next to impossible to sway them."

I nod like I understand, but I'm not sure I do. I squeeze the bloody towel in my hands. "Thanks for helping me. I've been a mess lately. I've been afraid to leave the house." It feels good to say it out loud.

"I understand your fear. It's perfectly reasonable to be afraid. We all are."

"Will's not."

"He hides it well with his big talk, but that's why he trains so much. It's why he volunteers for every mission."

"Cleis does too, doesn't he?"

"Yes, but Cleis goes for different reasons. With Cleis it's an obsession. I think he's just been at it so long he can't admit defeat. When Ecrin disappeared . . ." Her tiny hands scrunch into fists and she eases them back open. "I hoped he would settle down, and let someone else take over." Her mouth quivers, and she looks away. "I'm sure Ambrose told you about the Order?"

"Some. They believe the Quaadah are fakes."

"That's the gist of it. They were a group of the original Hahmi—the pure Hahmi. Sometime after the creators vanished, many of the original Hahmi left in search of them. It's said there was once a portal through which one could travel anywhere, presumably, but others say it was only a link between Earth and Ovohares Graa, their planet—Cleis could tell you more, I only know what little I overhear. Anyway, they left, and the rest of the Hahmi stayed behind. There was work to do, after all—clearly humanity can't self-regulate—and someone had to be here should the Quaadah return. It was those Hahmi who formed the Order."

"Then the Quaadah returned and killed everyone."

"Correct. These days, the original Hahmi are long gone, but the Order remains. They still follow the old ways, and believe the real Quaadah will save us all, but they're no longer waiting around. There have always been rumors that there's another portal, but no one's been able to find it, and *that* is Cleis's obsession."

"Maybe he found it and he's not actually missing." I say, hoping to lift her spirits, but she only frowns. I glance at the picture on her desk. "He could still be out there."

Anne nods. "I hope so." Her voice wavers like she's about to cry.

"What about Giric?" I say, blurting out the first thing that comes to mind.

Her eyes snap to mine. "What about him? Is he still harassing you?"

Suddenly I feel shy and I study my hands. Why did I have to bring up Giric? "He's . . ." I peer into her childlike face, wondering how much I should say, trying to judge how she'll react. Will she laugh like Will, or be dismissive like Alan and Ambrose? It's hard to reconcile her youthful appearance with her serious demeanor. She looks so fragile, but at the same time, there's a hardness in her. A core of steel.

She leans forward as if in moving closer she can hear my unspoken words.

"I think he threatened me when I came back after . . . after Will and I were attacked on Friday. He was waiting in the hall, just standing there in the dark."

"What did he say?"

"He just said 'take care,' but the look he gave me . . . It's like he was surprised to see me. Like he knew what happened, and in not getting killed I'd ruined his life, and now he means to do something about it."

She folds her arms over her chest, staring at nothing. Then her eyes focus and she straightens, crossing one knee over the other. "I'm sure it's just a misunderstanding, but I'll see what I can find out—quietly, of course. In the meantime, stay out of his way, and don't do anything rash."

I nod. Yeah, nothing rash. She doesn't need to know I broke into his room.

❀ ❀ ❀

"We're going to try something different," Will says from beneath the canopy of magnolia blossoms. "You can take off the blindfold."

"Oh, good. I get to watch you use my head as a punching bag?"

He smiles brilliantly. "No. We're going to take a break from the shadow-self."

"Because I suck at it?" I fling the blindfold to the grass.

Will frowns down at the cloth. "I never said that, but there are other things you need to learn."

"Like?"

"Stealth, for one. With the Quaadah, you only get one shot. They hear you coming, you're dead. You've got to move quickly. Silently. Watch."

He sprints between the trees, his feet barely touching the grass. The only sound is the slight hum of the fan and the buzz of tiny insects in the flowers. He loops back around and stops in front of me. "Now you."

I'm already exhausted, but I do as he asks. I hardly go two feet before he's yelling for me to stop.

"You're too tense. Contract your stomach but keep breathing. Let your legs be light, like springs. Bounce with me." He bends and straightens his knees, bobbing in place.

He looks ridiculous. "No way!" I can't help laughing.

"Come on. No one's watching."

I heave a giant sigh and imitate him, bobbing in the grass like an idiot.

"Well the gardener's watching, but he doesn't care."

"What!" I spin around, searching for the spy, but there's no one there.

He hoots laughter, slapping his knee. "Got you good. If you could've seen your face!" He wipes his eyes. "But come now, keep it up." He resumes bouncing. "Knees light. That's it. All right, give it another go."

I try again and again, and each time he shakes his head and waves his hand for me to start over. The sun is setting, its brilliant rays jab at my eyes through the branches.

"No. Stop. You're stomping. Can't you hear?"

I screech at him, startling a bird into flight. It's impossible. I'll never figure this out. So what if the Quaadah kill me. At least I won't have to do this anymore.

"You're trying too hard." He grabs my shoulders and shakes me lightly. "Loosen up, be light, and weightless. Remember? Go!"

I roll my eyes and take a deep breath. "Okay." Feet light, breath calm. I run.

"Yes! Much better!" I turn to see a wide, toothy grin swallowing his face.

"Finally! Can we stop now?"

He glances at his watch. "Fine. I guess since Anne's turned you on to those blood bags, you won't be doing much fleeing tonight."

"They're not so bad."

His lip curls. "I prefer the real thing. Even if it's risky." He shrugs, grinning again. "Probably because it's risky. I'm not cut out for domestic life." He looks off toward the setting sun, his face glum.

I think about telling him about the warehouse—he likes risks, maybe he could check it out—but I quickly change my mind. He'd want to know how I found out, and he'd only laugh again if I brought up my suspicions about Giric. I think about the dead guy—was he still up there? Probably not, or the whole house would reek by now. No. I'm on my own. Even if it means sneaking out to investigate alone. Panic blooms in my chest at the thought. Lightning doesn't strike the same place twice, right? What could go wrong?

Chapter 16

nne's words echo in my head as I sit behind the wheel of Ambrose's SUV. *Don't do anything rash.* And I haven't. In fact, I haven't done anything for the last three days but train, sleep, and drink blood from plastic bags. I can't stand it anymore. I can't wait for Anne. I need to act. Maybe I should ask Will to come along, but a quick survey of the garage reveals I'm too late. His car is gone. I'm on my own.

I pry one hand off the steering wheel, take a deep breath, and start the engine. It's loud in the dark. The headlights turn on automatically, flooding the garage, glaring off the taillights of the other vehicles, creating red eyes in the dark. It's been over eight years since I last drove a car, and the thought that I might have forgotten how has crossed my mind more than once. I can do this—as long as I keep to familiar roads and avoid the panic attack-inducing horrors of highways. I just have to cross the bridge. I can do this.

I ease out of the garage, down the drive, and onto the street. The road rolls by impossibly fast, and I step on the brake a little too hard and jerk against the seat belt. It's okay—deep breath. I force my foot off the brake and follow the signs to the

Burnside Bridge. The speedometer reaches fifteen, and I fight the urge to brake again.

A few minutes later, I'm creeping past twenty, and I give it a bit more gas. Driving isn't all that bad, at least not this late on a Sunday. Slowly, my shoulders relax, and my heart removes itself from my throat.

Somehow I've crossed the bridge, and I've passed through Chinatown and the Pearl. Sprawling warehouses spring up all around me, and the street is rutted with potholes and railroad tracks. Three blocks from my destination, I pull into a weed-strewn lot, crossing my fingers that nothing sharp lodges in my tires. A flat is the last thing I need.

Now that the car has stopped moving, and my anxiety over driving has subsided, I fully realize the insanity of what I'm about to do. It's not too late to go back. I could call Will, he might help. I reach for my phone in the cup holder. No. He'll be pissed. He forgave me for sneaking out last time, but now I'm a repeat offender. He'll escort me back, tell me I read too much, and lock me up. But hey, at least locked up I'd be safe . . . except that Giric has keys to the cells.

That settles it. I climb out, tuck my phone and keys into in my pockets, and tug up my hood. I pick my way through the weedy lot. The air stinks of burning plastic and hot metal. I doubt these fumes are safe, but I don't think lung cancer's a worry among Hahmi.

The blocks are short, and before long, an enormous brick and metal building looms across the street. It appears abandoned, the windows dark, the small parking strip deserted. Scraggly tufts of grass thrust up between cracks in the asphalt, and all around glass shards glint in the moonlight. The entrance is a pair of red doors held shut with a chain and padlock. The lock won't be a problem, but removing the chain will be loud.

My gaze drifts to the windows, none of them are at ground level. There's a broken one two stories up, but there's no easy way up. Will scaled an entire building with me on his back, but I haven't mastered that. I doubt I ever will. But could I jump to it?

"Forget your human limitations," I whisper, mocking Alan's stuffy English accent. I shove my hood back and focus on the narrow window ledge about twenty feet up. It's impossible, but I launch. It's like I'm made of lead. I manage maybe five feet before slamming into the metal siding with a deafening bang. I thump back to the choppy blacktop and scramble away, ducking into the shadows across the street.

Nothing moves. I wait for someone to come running out. I wait another minute, five, seven, then slink back and try again, this time with a longer run-up. It's no use. I flee to the shadows again. Crouched across the street, I consider the chain wrapped around the door handles. It won't be any louder than I've already been. I fish my lock picks from my pocket. I'll just pull the chain off, quick like a Band-Aid.

The lock pops in less than a minute, and I grip one end of the chain. Braced for the racket, I count to three and yank. The chain clatters free, and for the third time, I rush to the safety of the shadows, my heart hammering. I force myself to take twelve long, slow breaths before returning to the doors.

The hinges creak loudly—why am I even surprised?—but I've given up on stealth; I've already made enough noise to alert the entire world to my presence. It's obvious no one is here. Inside it's too dark to see much of anything. I pull my phone from my pocket, confirm the ringer's on silent, and hold it before me. It makes for a crappy flashlight—I should have upgraded to one of the newer phones with the fancy, blinding camera light—I'll put that on my list for next time. I'll just ask the sap working the counter which model is best for breaking and entering.

I jump at movement, but it's just the light reflecting off the steel railing of the observation deck overhead. The deck wraps around the whole building, and in the far corner, I can just make out a staircase leading up. I creep along the wall, feeling exposed. I should have brought my sword, though it's probably better I didn't. My meager ten days of training would be laughable against Giric's hundred plus years. Would I even hear him coming? I whirl around at the thought, but I'm alone.

Up ahead, a heavy steel door swims out of the dark. It's slightly ajar, and the light from my phone winks off a thick bolt lock. As I draw nearer, the caustic smell of bleach wafts out, burning my throat. I swing the door open. The odor intensifies, and I step inside, blinking back tears.

There's nothing to see, just an eight-by-twelve windowless room. The cement walls and floor are damp, as if every inch has been scrubbed. Nothing remains but an echo of unease. I snort. There's no such thing, but I feel . . . something. No. My mind's trying to attach something to nothing. So, someone cleaned, big deal.

The warehouse brightens as a vehicle pulls up outside. I whirl to face the open door, fumbling to snuff the light on my phone. Finally I give up and just stuff it into my pocket. My heart pounds, each beat screams *run*, but my legs won't obey. I stumble out of the little room. My eyes dart from the exit—the only exit—to the impossibly-high deck railing to the staircase at the opposite end of the warehouse. I stand frozen in deliberation for too long. Outside, the engine cuts off, a car door opens.

My time is up. My hands shake and I focus on the steel railing, bright in the light pouring in from outside. Beyond the door, feet crunch on broken glass.

Focus.

The sounds fade and the room drops away. I can do this. My muscles bunch, and I spring—but I can tell it's not good enough. I stretch my arms up, as if I can will myself higher, and somehow my hands close on cold metal—the lowest rung of the railing. My breath rushes out, and I bite the inside of my cheek to keep from laughing or screaming or both.

The ground spins, stretching out far below me and my stomach does a flip. Swallowing hard, I shut my eyes, and concentrate on the solidness of the metal under my palms. "I'm okay," I whisper, and I find it's true. I'm in no danger of falling, my arms aren't straining. I could hang here all day if I want.

A heavy jangling comes from the doorway—someone has picked up the chain. They're right outside the door. I can't breathe, can't move. The chain clatters back to the pavement and my paralysis breaks. In one adrenaline-fueled motion, I'm up and over the railing. I come down on the other side amid a cluster of massive steel drums. Amazingly, I don't make a racket or knock anything over, and I wedge myself in between the rail and two enormous drums.

I'm pretty pleased with my hiding place—that is, until the overhead lights snap on, flooding the entire building with sickly fluorescent light. Now all that's keeping me safe is meager shadows, my propensity for dark clothing, and the common rule that most people don't look up.

Giric steps into view, the heels of his shiny boots click on the cement. I roll my eyes; even his footwear is pretentious. He pauses in the middle of the room and turns in a slow circle, his eyes darting around. He spins on his heel, and while his back is to me, I flip up my hood and sink back against the cold steel. I hold my breath, hoping there's enough shadow to conceal me. With my eyes squeezed shut, I imagine I'm invisible, non-existent. It's laughable, but everyone keeps telling me to forget my human limitations.

Giric is on the stairs now, nearly silent, I can just make out the faint tap of his fancy boots on the metal. I redouble my efforts, quieting my breath, focusing on not being. Mind over matter, right?

I have no concept of how much time passes, but I open my eyes to the sound of feet shuffling on the concrete below. A man appears. At first my mind tries to see Giric, but it's not him, not even close. This guy is blonde, for one, and . . . there's something in the way he moves—I'm positive he's human. I probe his mind to be sure; there's nothing, but it's not quite the same as the nothing I've felt from Ambrose or Will. It's somehow emptier. Another person steps into view, then another. I count eight—no, ten. All of them blank-faced, one following the other in lockstep.

There's a loud thump as the entry doors close, and Giric reappears, tailing the procession. They file to the clean little room, then stop. The man in the lead pulls the door wide. I wrinkle my nose, recalling the noxious bleach fumes, but he doesn't seem to notice—none of them do. One by one they shuffle in, and after a furtive glance around, Giric slips in after them, pulling the door closed behind him.

I watch the door, my eyes fixed on the heavy lock on the outside. I could pop down and throw the bolt. I'd never have to worry about him again. My legs twitch, eager to get moving, but I wait, sure the door will open any second. It doesn't. Unease grips my stomach.

And then I hear muffled screams from behind the door. It sounds like a massacre in there, but why? My mind races in too many directions at once. I should help them, that would be the right thing to do, but part of me knows this is my chance: I have to lock him in while he's occupied. All the while, another part insists I have to get out now. But I'm frozen in place, paralyzed by the muted shrieks behind the heavy door, and I hate myself for being such a coward. I'm no better than Giric.

It doesn't occur to me that Giric might have a lookout until it's too late: a muffled footstep behind me, then a clammy hand clamps over my mouth, another around my arm, and I'm jerked out from between the barrels like I weigh nothing. I thrash, twisting wildly, but the arms lock, wrenching my elbows behind my back. The moment the hand comes off my mouth, my own screams fill the warehouse. I struggle, but it's no use, and I'm thrown over their shoulder. I get a view of their backside, clad in a rough grey robe, then they are running. I try to scream, but I can't get enough air for more than a harsh wheeze before we leap out of the broken window.

My teeth snap together as we land on the pavement outside, but my abductor doesn't hesitate. They're running again, full speed. I hope they trip on the uneven blacktop, then maybe I can get away, but it doesn't seem likely. We race past warehouses and fenced-in lots with no sign of slowing. Each change of direction seems random. I swear if I get out of this alive, I'll never sneak out again. I'll completely dedicate myself to training. I'll be the most obedient Hahmi ever.

At last we slow, my captor releases me, and I get my first look. The first thing I notice is her violet eyes. Just like mine. She's Hahmi, then? But there's something more, and for some reason, Ambrose's words from my dream clamor in my head. *Your life is but a borrowed thing. We will have it back.* My blood turns to ice. I can't move, I can't breathe. I shouldn't have left the house alone. I should've told Will. But I deserve whatever's coming with the way I just sat there. I should have at least tried to help those people.

She steps closer and I want to scream, but it wouldn't matter, there's no one around to hear. A long matted rope of white-blonde hair slips over one shoulder as she leans toward me. "I don't think you realize all you've nearly undone." Her voice is weird, feminine but strangely mechanical.

"Who—"

She presses one long finger against her lips. "Return to your house and speak of this to no one, not even Alan. I must speak with him directly."

"You know Alan? Please don't tell him I was here."

She grins, almost, maybe it's a sneer and I regret my words. Of course, she'll tell him now, then it's only a matter of time before Alan finds out the rest. Is breaking and entering a crime in the Hahmi world? It can't be that big of a deal, right? They wouldn't cut off my head for something this minor. Especially not when Giric's done much worse.

"That depends on you. I can keep a secret, if you can."

She's smiling now. I think she means to be comforting but something about her makes me uneasy. I'm almost certain she's not going to kill me, but I doubt she'll hold up her end of this deal. I nod, giving her my promise of silence. "Will you help them?" I tip my head in the direction of the warehouse.

She stiffens, drawing back a little, "It's too late for them. Now go."

She points behind me, and I follow the line of her bony finger. I'm shocked to see she's taken me back to Ambrose's SUV.

I whip around, meaning to ask how she knew I was here, how long she'd been watching, but she silences me with a sharp glance and a shake of her head. "Go, and remember, not a word. To act prematurely could devastate millions. There's already enough blood on your hands."

My cheeks grow hot and tears sting in my eyes. I step forward to say . . . what exactly? I don't know. That it wasn't my fault? That she was there too, and she'd done nothing?

Whatever I intended to say, it doesn't matter, she's already halfway down the block. A moment later, the darkness swallows her.

❄ ❄ ❄

As I pull into the garage, my hands are shaking so badly that I struggle to read the display on my phone. It's just past midnight; I've been gone over two hours. I enter the dark mudroom and return Ambrose's car key to its hook. A light is on in the library, and I hold my breath as I pass, placing my feet quietly, creeping up the stairs like a thief.

"Sasha?"

I spin and nearly tumble down the stairs.

Alan stands at the foot, his jaw set, eyebrows mashed together forming that weary line. "I asked that you not leave the house on your own. I know you're not accustomed to our ways, but it's for your safety. More go missing each day. Whole houses have been devastated—" He draws a deep breath. "I'm sorry. I don't mean to frighten you. I won't ask where you've been, but I do expect you to abide by the rules." His eyes soften. "Come now, don't look so downtrodden. This is your first offense. I'm willing to overlook it this once."

Some of the tension eases from my shoulders. First offense? Will hasn't ratted me out then. "I'm sorry, I—"

"Never mind that now. I have a spot of good news: the search party is returning. They should be back in a day or so. That should lift your spirits."

My heart flutters, and I almost topple down the steps again. I clutch the railing. "Did they find the others? Did they find Cleis?"

He shakes his head. His throat works as if he wants say more, but he only smiles dolefully.

I should feel comforted—Ambrose is coming back—but all I can think of is the warehouse, those screams. I'm not even sure what I saw or what I'm not allowed to say. I guess I'm quiet for too long, because Alan is looking at me with concern. I throw out the first thing that comes to mind. "How's Anne?"

"It's difficult for her, but she'll survive. She's been dreading this for centuries. Not that it makes the news any easier to bear. We take the good with the bad." He shrugs like he's trying to heave the weight from his shoulders and turns back toward the library. "Good night."

I hope Anne will be okay, but I know she won't, not for a while. She couldn't be. For her to lose Cleis, to lose someone she loves so deeply—and it's clear she loves him. Truly, wholly. I can't even imagine loving someone like that. I've never allowed myself to love anyone. It hardly seems fair for Ambrose to be returning. My stomach tightens at the thought. In a few—days? hours?—Ambrose will be here.

Hope expands in my chest. It's such an odd feeling after the doom of the past few days, but I can't kill it. I run the last few steps to the bedroom feeling stupidly, selfishly happy.

Deep in the pit of my stomach, beneath the airy giddiness, tendrils of unease twist and unfurl. Hope, like love, is just a four-letter word that ends in misery.

Chapter 17

The soles of Ecrin's boots make no sound as she sprints across the uneven pavement; a block away, the engine of the girl's black SUV revs then fades into the distance. Light spills from the open warehouse door onto the warped blacktop, and she slows as she reaches the silver Mercedes out front. After a quick glance around, Ecrin stoops by the back tire. Metal winks in the light, and as she stands, the tire begins to hiss.

She approaches the open door slowly as if she expects someone will jump out, but once inside, she walks confidently to the far door where she pauses, eyes closed, head cocked. The screams have stopped, there's only a soft shuffle, a whisper of feet, just below the range of human hearing, but Ecrin isn't human. Something like a smile flickers at her lips as she finds the heavy bolt on the outside of the door still unlocked.

Behind her, a man watches just beyond the entrance. His boots are gone and the harsh yellow light dulls his chestnut curls. He clutches a weathered four-foot fence plank in one hand and watches as Ecrin cracks the door open. Ecrin's eyes narrow against the caustic stench of bleach, and the shuffling sound grows louder. Her shoulders straighten, her hand dips into her robe.

Her hand freezes, the door open hardly more than a crack, the sound behind the steel door is more of a scuffing. She yanks the door open. Just inside, a blood-crusted man hangs from the low ceiling, swinging slightly, his shoes softly brushing the cement. Beyond him, everything is red and wet and still.

Ecrin whips around, but too late; a loud bang echoes through the warehouse. Her eyes center on the double doors, now closed. Outside, there's the scrape of wood on metal followed by the purr of an engine turning over, the squeal of tires on pavement. Her eyes go wide and she bolts for the doors, throwing her shoulder against the metal. There's no give, but she rams the door twice more, her face twisted in anger. Then her eyes brighten, and she races for the stairs and the broken window on the upper floor.

❖ ❖ ❖

A loud voice wakes me and my skin tightens with goose bumps. I swallow hard. It was just a dream, but I can still see the blonde woman grinning at me through the window of a black van— the same woman from the warehouse. Her words, what had she said? Was she yelling? It doesn't matter; the dream is already fading.

I grab my phone from the shelf above my head, wincing at the brightness of the display. Three in the morning. Why am I even up? I shake my head and lie back down.

"Hello?" A voice calls from down stairs. This is definitely not a dream. I throw back the covers, grab my sword, and hurry out of the closet. Maybe it's Ambrose and his team—Alan said they were on their way.

I rush into the hall and skid to a stop at the top of the stairs. In the foyer below, the woman from my nightmare—the same woman from last night—stares up at me, her matted blonde hair spilling out from beneath her hood. A chill runs down my spine. I want to run, but I'm frozen in place. I draw a deep breath; there's nothing to be afraid of. She's on our side—one of us.

Will appears below, barely decent in briefs and a short bathrobe, and Anne is right on his heels, but she stops short upon seeing the hooded blonde figure, and her face falls.

"Ecrin?" Anne's voice floats up from the foyer. Anne's tone implies she wants to say more, her eyes dart around the room as if she expects to find someone else—Cleis perhaps?

Will's eyes widen. "We thought you were dead. Where—what have you—"

"What's all the racket?" Alan bursts into the foyer, a burgundy smoking jacket cinched around his waist, his hair standing at odd angles. He spots Ecrin, and his face breaks into a brilliant smile that doesn't quite smooth the worry line between his eyebrows.

I watch from the top of the stairs, reluctant to join them. My attention drifts back to the hooded woman, only to realize she's staring at me again, a malicious glint in her eyes.

I suppress a shudder and force myself to smile. It's all in my head. I did as she asked, I didn't say a word to anyone, she has to know that, right? But, will she tell Alan what I'd been up to?

"Hello, Ecrin." Alan stands awkwardly, head cocked. His eyes are distant, and it seems like he's looking through Ecrin rather than at her.

I'm contemplating sneaking back into my room, when Alan notices me on the stairs and waves me down. I creep into the foyer, keeping my eyes off Ecrin, and slip in next to Will.

Alan turns back to Ecrin. The worry line is deeper than ever. "Are you ready to tell me what's going on?"

Ecrin nods. "The situation is grave, and I will only discuss matters with the heads of house."

Will butts in, his eyes darting between Ecrin and Alan. "What situation? Don't you trust your own house?"

Alan waves a hand, silencing him, and Will's jaw bunches. Alan turns back to Ecrin. "I'll call an emergency meeting." Alan's gaze shifts around the circle. "Please. None of this is to be repeated. Not yet anyway." With a slight bow, Alan excuses himself from the room.

Will huffs beside me and mutters, "It's not like I can tell anyone what's going on anyway. I'm being kept in the dark in my own house."

"Will, it's just a precaution." Anne says, "I'm sure everything will be cleared up after the meeting." Will looks like he's about to say something, and Anne cuts him off, turning her attention to Ecrin. "Can I get you anything? Have you fed?"

Ecrin, says nothing and only shakes her head.

Anne appears irritated, but it doesn't show in her voice. "Will you be staying with us? May I take your robe? We could wait in the study."

Ecrin blinks once with reptilian slowness, and her mouth pulls into a sneering smile. "I think it's best to wait for discussion until Alan returns."

Anne's eyes catch mine for an instant, and I detect a flash of anger before she dons a friendly smile once more. "Yes, of course."

We all stand awkwardly silent. Will and Anne seem to be trying to communicate, unsuccessfully, through blinks and stares, and Ecrin turns to the window by the door, overlooking the front walk. I'm just glad she's no longer focused on me. Now's my chance. I should creep back to my room while no one's paying attention. It's not like I'll find anything out anyway. Ecrin only wants to talk to important people, so what am I waiting around for?

I catch movement down the hall near the entrance to the mudroom. Giric peeks around the corner. He glares at Will and Anne's back, then his gaze shifts to Ecrin and his eyes widen, almost like he's scared. Should I say something? He's obviously sneaking around. He catches me watching him and darts back into the mudroom.

I look back at the group. Anne yawns, and Will sighs. Ecrin is staring at me, a hungry look in her eyes. I try not to shiver.

"I forgot something in the atrium," I mumble to no one in particular. It takes everything I have to maintain a casual pace down the hall. I focus on the whisper of my stockinged feet on the cool tile. The mudroom is dark, almost too dark to see, but I leave the light off. If Giric is outside, I don't want him to know I'm coming.

I ease the door open and step out into the garage. As the door shuts behind me, a soft whoosh cuts through the air. There's a cold sting along my neck, and I pitch forward, but instead of falling, the room flips end over end, like I'm tumbling in a dryer. My arms won't move, and the hard cement rushes up to meet me.

❈ ❈ ❈

Thank you for reading *Dead Like Stars*, book one of the Bloodlife series. I hope it was as much fun to read as it was to write.

As an independent author, I'm not backed by a marketing team nor do I have the influence or advantage of a traditional publisher; I depend on readers like you to help spread the word.

If you enjoyed *Dead Like Stars*, here's how you can help:

- Post a review on Amazon—It can be short or long. Anything helps
- Tell your friends
- Share on places like Facebook and Twitter
- Subscribe to my mailing list at AnastasiaPoirier.com for updates on book two and future releases
- Review and add *Dead Like Stars* to lists on Goodreads in categories like Vampire, Urban Fantasy, or Female Protagonist.

Thank you!
Anastasia Poirier

Still with me? Great! You're the best. Keep reading for a free preview of *Darkling Like Stars*, book two in the Bloodlife series.

Darkling Like Stars

Insects with feet and teeth like razors scurry along my body, stabbing into my eyelids, lips, toes. I try to open my eyes, try to shake them off, but nothing moves. I want to scream but I can't draw a breath. The more I attempt to struggle, the more agitated the bugs become. Their needle legs shred my skin, stabbing like a million pins. They multiply. Thousands of them, scurrying back and forth.

My eyes pop open. I wince against harsh white light and squeeze them shut again. Tears ooze out, matting in my lashes. At last, cool air rushes down my throat, filling lungs that feel wet and heavy like soaked denim.

I try to raise my arms, but I meet resistance. My eyes open again, slowly this time. Light radiates from everywhere, bouncing off smooth metallic walls. I lift my head and grit my teeth against another wave of biting, stabbing pain, but it's not as bad now. I glance down my body, relieved to see there are no insects. There never were. That part, at least, was a dream or hallucination or some combination of the two. I breathe through the pain. At least it confirms I'm alive.

I'm still wearing my pajamas from . . . was that earlier today? Last week? My shirt is stiff, caked with dried blood—my blood? My neck itches the way wounds do when they heal, and again I try to raise my arms and meet resistance, but now I can see why: three metallic restraints—one across my shoulders, another across my waist and wrists, and one across my shins. They fasten me to what might be an operating table. What happened? I remember the dark mudroom and stepping out into the even darker garage. A flash of cold pain. Giric?

"Hello?" My voice wavers, and I wince against the burning pain in my throat. It's like I swallowed broken glass. My left hand aches dully. I can't see far enough to know why, but there's a blood bag suspended from a metal stand and a trail of plastic tubing, so I assume there's an IV jabbed in there. I stare at the bag, at the deep red fluid, and now I can feel it: the slow, cool stream dripping into my hand is torture. Relief doled out drop by drop. I want buckets—rivers of blood.

The wall slides open with a hiss and someone enters, an abstract form pushing a gleaming metallic cart. A moment later, there's a rush of air as the wall closes. The figure is covered head to toe in a white material that throws back the light. It looks like a form-fitting space suit. He pauses and rolls back the cover on the cart, exposing a bulky machine with a glass screen. Several violet icicle-like sticks protrude from a metallic cup on top. They glow, pulsing almost as brightly as the lights.

The cart is in motion again, tinkling softly as it rolls across the floor, then it, and the figure, disappear behind me. It has to be Giric, but what's with the outfit?

The conclusion isn't pretty. He doesn't want to kill me, not yet anyway. I shoot a glance at the IV tubing trickling blood into me. He's going to torture me. He wouldn't want to get blood all over his fancy clothes, and he's too conceited to wear scrubs. Who knew designer hazmat suits were a thing?

I tilt my head back as far as my restraints allow, ignoring the tingling itch at my throat, straining to see what he's doing; it's impossible. "Alan will know you're behind this. I told him all about you," I lie. "If you let me go, I'll say it wasn't you." I hold my breath, hoping he'll listen.

He says nothing.

A hand comes down on my forehead, cold and clammy like a snake. I jerk against the restraints, whipping my head back and forth. The hand tightens, and I'm sure my skull will crack under the pressure.

There's a loud pop, then a low buzz fills the room. A drill? Saw? My imagination kicks into overdrive, my breath coming in too-close gasps. I'm going to hyperventilate. Is that even possible for Hahmi? I squeeze my eyes shut. I can get out of this. I just need to think of the right thing to say.

The buzzing thing touches my temple, and I yelp. It drags along my scalp, just above my ears, first on one side, then the other, but there's no pain. Hanks of my hair drop around me, tickling my ears.

Not a drill. Clippers? He's saving my head? But he only gets as far as my temples. The buzzing stops, and he releases my forehead, leaving a cold phantom handprint that seeps into my skin. I shake my head, and more of my hair falls to the table.

"Giric, you don't have to do this." It's a stupid thing to say. It never works in movies; it certainly isn't going to work in real life.

He appears at my side, a silhouette against the blinding light. His hand shoots out, grasps my jaw, and a hard gag is forced between my teeth and secured behind my head. I cough around it, retch, and almost puke before my stomach settles.

Giric leans over me, momentarily blocking the light, and I see fully violet eyes. It's not Giric at all; it's not even Hahmi. It looks at me like I'm something to be studied, like it wants to hurt me. I can't help but wonder what it sees when it looks at me. My screams are muffled by the gag. It raises one finger to its lips, its mouth twitches, and then it recedes back into the light.

A cold, damp cloth swabs my temples and the center of my forehead, and my stomach tightens at the strong antiseptic smell. It reminds me of hospitals and pain and my father's lies. *She was playing volleyball, Doctor*, he would say, his eyes boring into mine, promising worse if I dared divulge the real reason for that day's gushing wound.

I buck against the restraints, knowing it won't do any good. I'm trapped. Already my jaw is aching from the gag. I was afraid of what Giric might do, but this is entirely different. I could have reasoned with Giric—maybe—but the Quaadah? My mind fills with a million images from every *X-Files* episode I've ever seen.

The wall hisses open and another form enters, joining the first behind me. Cold hands fall to either side of my head, and one of the creatures—the one who gagged me? The new one? I can't tell—steps to my side. Three glowing, tapered rods, like translucent knitting needles, poke out from one pale, spidery hand. In its other it holds what looks like a rubber mallet.

I don't want to know what these things are for, but my mind is already supplying images of lobotomies. Can Hahmi brains heal? "Please. No," I say, but my words are mush around the gag. I struggle against the restraints, trying to twist free from the hands holding my head.

One captor says something to the other, its voice cold and clinical, the language harsh with too many vowels, and the hands holding me shift down to the sides of my head, clamping around my ears.

No matter how hard I fight, I can't move. Cool fingers probe along my forehead, pressing, slithering along the bone, searching. Then the fingers are replaced by a sharp point in the center of my forehead, and a chill slides down my spine. A constant whining *No, no, no* is all I can say, all I can think. I can't slow my breath; it comes faster and faster. Then I'm choking on the spit collecting at the back of my throat. I can't close my mouth enough to swallow. I can't breathe. At any moment I hope to see busy black dots that will take me down into unconsciousness, but they won't come.

There's one thing I failed to consider about this new life: sure, I may be impervious to death, but that just means I can be tortured forever.

❧ ❧ ❧

Want more? Sign up for my mailing list at AnastasiaPoirier.com for updates on *Darkling Like Stars*, book two of the Bloodlife series. Your email address will never be sold or shared, and you can unsubscribe any time.

Thank you for reading. If you enjoyed *Dead Like Stars*, please help spread the word: post a review and tell your friends.